HEXES & HOUNDS

BEAUTIFUL BEASTS ACADEMY

KIM FAULKS

MILA YOUNG

Kim: I'm dedicating this one to the creatives and the witches, to those left off-center, the 3am risers who burn their light a little brighter. My people. This one is for you.
Mila: To all my readers...thank you for always being there for me. Love you guys

Join our Kila Foung reader group by clicking on the image below and joining the shenanigans!

Grab your FREE
book and start
the Beautiful
Beasts Academy
Series today!

Love is complicated.
But then so is a stake through the heart.
There's a curse that runs through the Blackthorne Wolves.
Gnarled and Ancient. Unbreakable, they say.
It started with the Witches and now it's spread like a
disease, infecting Wolves...
And now Vampires.

Livingstone Vampires.

Mom's frantic calls led me to the Blood Moon Academy, a
dangerous place for any Immortal.
I found dad there, chained like a beast, filled with rage.
And as everything changes around me, I'm sent a command
from the Ancient...it's time to step up.
Time to be the Vampire my kind needs to me be.
Understudy. Vampire. Daughter.

I don't know who I am anymore.

But I'll search for answers.
I'll do it all with the Wolves, my best friend and my
bodyguard at my side.
And as the curse reaches out and marks my skin, I start to
question everything.
How far will I go for love?
And, how far will love go for me?

CHAPTER ONE

DARK CORNERS AND STEEL CHAINS

"I swear, you smack into the back of me one more freaking time and I'm gonna lose my shit," Ava snarled as we crouched in the bushes.

I lifted my gaze to the red windows in the cathedral looking building, towering against a midnight sky. "You sure this is the place?"

Nero turned to glance at me and gave a nod. "This is the place."

Energy hummed through the air. It crawled up my leg and spilled over my shoulders, sucking me in like a lover's greedy kiss.

"I don't like this place. It feels *wrong*," Ava murmured beside me.

"It's supposed to feel like that," Nero added. "It's a warding spell. They want you to be scared enough to leave."

"It's doing a damn good job." Ava rubbed her arms.

"Don't be scared." Chuck stood straight and tall, the top of his head peeking out of the bushes. "I won't let anything happen to you."

"We get in, get your dad and get out," Bond growled as he stared at the rust colored stained glass windows.

The Blood Moon Academy looked every bit as fucking terrifying as the name. If it wasn't for my dad, I'd never step foot in the place. But love was stronger than fear—I glanced beside me—and friendship was just as powerful.

"Agreed," I answered and took a step forward, leading the others as I left the bushes behind and made for the wide steps of the Academy hall.

Witches were feared.

Witches were hated.

Witches didn't play well with others.

And yet here I was, handing myself and my friends to them on a damn platter.

"Seems too quiet." Ava scanned the line of trees as she stepped up to the pathway.

It was too quiet. Too cold. Too dark. Too...*everything*.

My nerves jumped and twitched. A warm hand grasped mine as Ava flinched and looked toward the door. "I'm scared," she muttered. "So, you're holding my damn hand."

I took the steps slowly, jostling to the side as Bond pressed against me, and then Nero.

Ava pushed back, Chuck bumped against her until we all stumbled and clattered like a herd of damn elephants.

"Stop," Bond growled.

"You stop," Ava snarled.

I took the next step on my own, leaving them all behind to fight it out amongst themselves, and reached for the door handle. Pain tore through my fingers, like a thousand volts shot through my hand.

But the pain was swallowed as fast as it came, and I twisted the handle and then pushed.

Darkness and silence waited for me inside.

The thud of my boots echoed and then mingled with the others as I stepped through the doorway. There was no sound from anyone, no...*feel* of anyone here.

"We're alone," Bond growled as I made my way through the foyer and turned into what looked like an elaborate sitting area.

I skimmed over the outline in the darkness and stepped closer. "We are alone," I murmured.

"Not exactly," a strange male's voice replied.

The *flick* of a light sounded in the space.

An amber flame followed, turning crimson in an instant.

A Warlock sat with one leg draped over an armrest of a plush chaise sofa in the middle of the room.

His red shirt gaped open, exposing a muscled chest as he flicked the lighter and then extinguished the flames. Dark eyes met mine as he lifted his gaze. "Morwenna Livingstone, I've been expecting you."

"My dad...I'm here for him," I demanded, and then swallowed hard.

Dark eyes burned with secrets. He smiled as he flicked the lighter, casting a faint red glow around the room. "Hmmm, see there's a problem with that."

"What kind of problem?" Chuck growled behind me.

But the Warlock didn't answer Chuck, in fact it was as though he didn't see him at all.

Flick.

Flick.

Flick.

The ignition made my undead heart clench with fear.

And out of the darkness behind him came movement. The blood red hue from the flames danced across a familiar face.

"Judas?" I murmured as he stopped at the Warlock's shoulder and stared at me. "What are you doing here?"

"Yes, Judas," murmured the Warlock. "I think it's time you told your Vampire friend all the juicy Blackthorne secrets. Let her know what a bad Wolf you really are."

Judas's stricken gaze met mine as he uttered two words I'd dreaded hearing. "I'm sorry."

Bond and Nero were silent beside me, but it was Ava who growled, and it was Ava who stepped forward. "You're sorry? You left us to die while the Demon's attacked the Academy dance. You're not sorry, you're an asshole."

Judas just nodded. "I deserve that. I didn't want to leave. I had to."

I couldn't deal with this, not now. I swallowed hard and tore my gaze from the silver shine of his eyes.

Flick.

"My father. He's here and I want him back."

The Warlock stopped flicking the lighter and leaned forward. I caught the wave of his hand in the darkness before soft amber lights illuminated the room from the corners. I could see him now, wide brown eyes, chiseled jaw. He looked like any other guy. But when he pushed against the soft red sofa and rose to his feet, I felt the sting of the magical connection instantly.

"That can't happen, Morwenna." He drew me in like a predator with careful long strides. "I know you're upset. I know you're scared. But this isn't the time. Do you understand what I'm telling you?"

Goosebumps raced along my skin with his deep baritone voice.

The Wolves blurred, taking Ava and Chuck with them. All I saw was seduction wrapped up in the skin of a man. "Go home, Morwenna. Go home and worry no more."

I shook my head, entranced by the brush of his fingers on my arm. Judas flinched, silver glinting eyes fixed on the movement of this man's touch. I couldn't quite think...*why was I here?*

"You look tired," the Warlock murmured. "So much has happened for you. You could almost walk right out of those doors and go back home. You could almost visit with your Mom, take care of her. Tell her Dante is perfectly fine. He's on a business trip and there's nothing to worry about."

My lips parted, the rush of a breath followed. There was something sweet and musty in the room, a scent I hadn't picked up before. And with the fragrance, came that rush of dark power inside.

She was still there, the woman in black, even after the diamonds had turned to dust and the Demons were gone. I could feel her, watching, waiting, making her presence known, just like she had then.

The flare of power was like the crack of a whip inside me, tearing through the foggy hold over my mind. I wrenched my arm from his touch and stumbled backwards. I saw him now, saw him for all his cruel, malignant desires. "Don't touch me," I warned. "And get the Hell outta my head. I want my father, and if you don't take me to him now, I'll tear your precious Academy to the ground."

The darkness rose inside me, searing along my bones, slipping under my skin. The floor underneath me trembled, and the lights in the corner of the room dimmed.

The Warlock glanced to the lights, as behind him Judas took a slow step forward, muttering, "I warned you, Keir."

I closed the distance and curled my lips. The Warlock wasn't the only predator in the room. "Give me my father."

The walls trembled, paintings on the wall bounced, and then slammed back again.

"She will spill blood, Warlock," Chuck warned. "She will desecrate every room of this place until you give him back to us, and I'll help her do it. We will not stop...for anything. Until we leave with Dante Livingstone."

"Keir," Judas warned, never once taking his eyes from me.

There was a shake of the Warlock's head, and that was enough for the rage trapped inside me to rear once more.

Unforgiving. Raw and feral.

Power swept through the room. The Warlock's eyes widened, his breath caught. There was a slight shake of his head. "What is that?" he murmured. "That power, that's not just Vampire power."

"That's not *just* a Vampire," Ava cautioned next to me. "Now I suggest you call whoever you need to call and let her dad go before she gets really pissed."

Nero and Bond said nothing, only stared at Judas.

"You don't want to do this," Keir warned with a shake of his head. "You don't want to see your father like...not the way he is."

A jolt of terror shot up my spine. "What do you mean, *the way he is?* He's my father."

Chuck's low, savage growl gave me strength. I curled my lips and bared my teeth. "Take me to him...*now.*"

Keir cut a glare to Judas, who just swallowed.

I'm sorry, the Alpha's words echoed in my head. He wasn't sorry, he'd been caught. There was a fucking difference.

The Warlock gave a small nod, dark eyes glinted with truth and terror. "Don't say I didn't warn you."

And with that he turned toward a large doorway that no doubt led further into the building. I saw this place then. The wooden walls, the bare room, the feeling of *emptiness.* I glanced to Ava, and then followed. We all did. Heavy foot-steps resounded, filling the hallway as we made our way deeper into the Academy. The walls were made of dark wood, lights dim, everything seemed so bleak.

"This place isn't a school, it's a damn morgue. Where is everyone?" Ava murmured.

"It's Beltane," Keir murmured and glared over his shoul-der. "Not that I expect you to care about our customs."

"The Fire of Bel," Ava murmured. "I know it, just figured there'd be more...you know...celebrating."

Keir tore his gaze away, instead he strode deeper into the darkened hallway. "There would be if there was some-thing to celebrate."

His sudden somber mood was unusual. I knew Witches were dangerous, knew they were to be feared and a second ago in the living room he was every bit of the formidable presence I thought he'd be. But something had changed. The Warlock had become this quiet, bruised man, and I didn't know how to read him.

He stepped through a walkway at the end of the hall and into a room that sank in the middle of the floor. It was a ramp that dropped underneath the floorboards. One wave of the Warlock's hand and the room was flooded with the same soft amber glow which stretched to the stairs reaching into the dark below.

I wanted to turn to the others, to reach out for Ava's hand, but I didn't. I clenched my fist, determined to do this on my own.

"Mor, *please* listen to me," Judas started.

"Why?" I snapped. "Why listen, why believe a thing you say? You won't be getting another opportunity to betray me again."

I turned then, and followed the Warlock as he stepped

off the ramp and onto the stairs. Heavy steps thudded, echoing around me, and that sweet, musty scent seemed to rise from the earth as I followed.

Careful now, a woman's voice floated through my mind.

A frigid draft swept across me from the room below.

I gripped the railing and blinked into the gloom, until a warm amber glow spread out below us. Glass jars glinted and sparkled under the glow. It was some kind of workroom. Potions crammed the benches. Dried herbs and flowers hung from ropes tied overhead. I cut my gaze around the room, searching for movement, and kept stepping. But there was no one, not a Witch or my father.

Heavy boots thudded on the packed earth floor as Keir stepped down into the room. I listened to the others fill the room behind me.

"I'm asking you one last time, Morwenna." Keir turned to meet my gaze. "Don't do this. Leave your father here, with us...with the ones who can—"

"Kill him?" I took a step closer meeting his gaze.

"Help him," he answered quietly.

"Mor," Judas murmured. Nero and Bond never moved aside, making a barrier between us. His brow narrowed, confusion swept in, still he tried to get through to me. "Listen to Keir, this isn't what you think it is. Your dad..." He glanced to the Warlock, but instead of subservience, a battle raged within the Alpha's soul. "He's sick. He's sick and he needs help."

I shook my head. Sick from what? The diamonds had been shattered, every other Vampire had their strength returned, even the Ancient. There was only...*me,* who still carried after effects. I'd checked the other Vampire bloodlines, I'd checked those who'd gone rogue. I'd turned over every stone I could find and made sure those who remained were strong once more.

So, there was no reason for Dad to be here. "I want to see. I *demand* to see."

The Warlock turned ashen under the amber lights, he straightened his spine, and then turned to stride down a narrow hallway that jutted out from the room. Lights glowed along the stony walls. The cold seemed to reach out from the walls, and somewhere along the hallway the rattle of chains followed.

I jerked my gaze toward the sound. My steps slowed, boots scraped the hard floor as the *clink* and *gnash* of steel links mingled together. My heart gave a slow *thud,* and the sound filled my ears.

A grunt came from a room up ahead. Pale light barely reached from under the door, but it was still there. Something moved inside that room, something that grunted and snarled. Something that tested the links on the chains with a *snap,* not once...but over and over.

And over.

I stopped in the middle of the hallway. They had a beast in there, torturing him...terrifying him. But the more I stared into those dark eyes the more I saw something *familiar.*

"I tried to warn you," Keir murmured. "He's not just your father, Mor...*he's dangerous.*"

"Daddy?" The word slipped from my lips. I saw him now...saw the man behind the monster.

My steps were a blur as I charged forward and grabbed the door handle. "Daddy...*Daddy!* I'm here. I'm coming."

"Morwenna...*wait!*" Judas roared as I gripped the handle and turned.

Power swept over me like a hurricane as the lock gave

way under my hand and the door swung inwards. I stumbled inside and stilled. Energy swirled around the room, dangerous, consuming energy that glowed and shone and swept in circles around a man tied to a chair in the middle if the room.

Dark, haunting, demented eyes stared back at me from the beast in chains.

His hands clenched the ends of the armrests until his knuckles turned white. Clothes had torn to shreds exposing his chest all the way to his waist. Black veins ran like whip marks underneath pale skin. I flinched as Judas' hand gripped mine.

But still I couldn't look away.

Not from the long white fangs.

Or from the way he snapped his body forward, testing the chains time and time again.

"I'll kill you," he sneered. "Come closer...come closer and I'll tear you apart."

The words were a knife in the middle of my chest as I stared at the man who once smiled at me across his desk. "Daddy..."

"That's not your Dad." Judas turned to me. "Not really. He's just a beast. An animal. He's sick, Morwenna. He's sick and he doesn't know how to fix this."

"That's why he came here." Keir stepped closer, drawing my gaze. "To the Blood Moon Coven. That's why he came to see our High Priest, Tagar Lutherian."

"You...*you people did this to him?*" I wrenched my gaze to Judas and the lying Warlock behind him. "*You did this to my father!*"

CHAPTER TWO

THE TRUTH WON'T ALWAYS SET YOU FREE

"No." Judas clasped my wrist and dragged me outside the dungeon. "You need to listen to me." He cast a panicked gaze to Chuck and then the others. "There's a sickness running through the most powerful of the supernatural lines. It started with the Witches, and then the Wolves."

He couldn't hold my gaze. Instead he stared at the cold stony walls.

"What do you mean sickness?"

"It affects the men, as far as we know," Judas murmured. "Turns them into monsters, makes them do things they can't control."

Sadness was etched into every word. He grabbed my hand, dragging me with him. "It's not safe here for you. Not with him."

I wanted to fight and thrash, to pull my hand from his and run into that room...*no, that cell,* once more. My heart gave another heavy *thud* and agony followed, tight and constricting, like a belt across my chest cinching tighter.

That was my father. The words tore through my head as

an unmerciful scream swallowed the thunder of footsteps, shattering my heart.

"That—" Chuck grabbed Keir's arm and wrenched the Warlock around to face him. "*That*...that *thing* in there is *not* Dante."

"It is," Keir growled, meeting the warriors terrifying stare. "You know it is. You are his bodyguard, right? You must've seen he was getting sick."

Chuck shook his head and turned, finding my gaze. Agony filled his eyes, there was a flicker of something...panic...*failure.*

"Did you know?" I murmured. "Did you see anything?"

"I thought he was just tired, snapping and one time he —" His eyes darkened with the memory, before he continued. "He's been under a lot of pressure. Your assignment from the Ancient. The Vampires being sick, and the other families ready to knife him in the back. I..."

"You protected him," Keir answered. "You made excuses. You overlooked. But there was no reason for you to know warrior, not until the night of the dance, when the Dragon's Tears were shattered. The power tore through every Vampire, and restored their power. But it changed Dante, it...bought whatever was trying to dig its claws into him rushing to the surface."

I closed my eyes as a wave of guilt hit me. Someone touched my arm, reassuring me. It could've been Nero, or Ava. I didn't know...or care. In this moment I was alone in my terror, unhinged and untethered.

Until silence made me open my eyes.

Chuck was a statue. Dark eyes glinted with something akin to madness as he dropped his hand from the Warlock's arm and stepped backwards.

A sickening howl of rage came from the hallway. Chuck

flinched, but he didn't turn toward the howl, only stared at the Witch.

"It's not safe for you here, Morwenna." Keir made for the potions room. "You need to leave, and the farther you stay from the Blood Moon Academy, the better. We'll take care of your father, do our best with the tonics and the sedation spells. But it seems the closer you are to him...the more violently he reacts."

I hurried after the Witch, trying to make sense of what he was saying. "I don't understand... Why? I should stay here. I should be the one taking care of him."

Keir stopped at the base of the stairs and turned. "I think Judas is the best one to answer your questions."

Judas? The betrayal still stung. I gripped the railing and climbed the stairs, but I still couldn't stop myself from listening for the Alpha behind me as I climbed all the way to the empty room of the Academy once more.

Judas stepped closer and reached for my hand, but I just shook my head and stepped away. I stared at his fallen posture, the way his shoulders dropped, and felt an ache in my chest.

"You don't understand," Judas began,

"Then help me understand," I snapped.

"Mor," Nero started.

"No," I growled. "No, Nero. I deserve the truth."

"You do," Judas added. "That's why I can't tell you."

And that ache bloomed into cold, hard anger.

"But I can show you," he finished. "It's the only way you'll understand."

"I don't think that's a good idea," Nero warned. "I don't think she's ready."

I flinched with the words. *They knew? They all knew?*

Judas seize my gaze and answered. "She's going to need to be."

His gaze shifted from me to Ava and Chuck, and then he turned and marched down the dark corridor. Nero turned, and Bond motioned with his head to follow.

"Mor?" Ava said softly. "What can I do?"

"Go back to the Academy with Chuck," I murmured. "This is something I need to do on my own."

"Mor, I don't think you should," Chuck rumbled.

But I was tired of the anger and the terror. I was tired of lugging around the guilt and shell-shocked disbelief of what had happened. I still fully didn't understand it. "I need...answers to the diamonds...to everything."

Judas looked to Keir.

"That's well above my powers," the Warlock muttered.

"Then I demand to see someone else," I growled and that hunger inside me rumbled beneath my skin.

There was a panicked glance from the Warlock to Judas before he answered. "Fine. I'll make the request, but I can't guarantee an outcome."

I gave a nod. If that was all I was going to get, then I'd accept it...*for now*.

"Chuck, take care of Ava. I'll be back when I can."

Ava rushed forward and hugged me. "Text me every thirty minutes or I'll assume the worst and come for you, you too *Wolf*." She glared at Judas.

I hugged her back, and fought the urge to smile. "Thanks, and I believe it."

She pulled away and stepped down from the front steps of the Academy, giving me one glance over her shoulder before she followed Chuck back the way we came to the black Mercedes parked on the shoulder of the road.

"You ready?" Judas murmured.

I sucked in a hard breath and then gave a nod. I followed the Alpha, along with Bond and Nero, all the way to a parking lot behind the towering front building of the Blood Moon Academy. In the darkness, far off in the distance, fires burned. "What is that?"

"That, is how Witches celebrate Beltane," Judas murmured.

I felt distant from everyone, from everything. Night cloaked the surrounding landscape, and the emotions inside me reminded me of what Dad had become. It crashed into me like endless waves.

Nero stepped closer, his warmth brushing against my arm. I wanted to recoil from him. I hurt him, just as he hurt me. I wanted to slap his face, to betray him...just so he knows how it feels to be betrayed. Instead I just stepped to the side, putting distance between us.

Tears blurred the darkness.

"Grandma would say tears shed for others were a sign of strength," Bond said.

I turned toward him, his words rolling over in my mind. "Really? Dad always told me to cry is a sign of a mortal."

"And by mortal, he means weak I take it?" Nero murmured.

Mortal. Weakness. He said anything other than the cold, stoic nature of the Vampire was something to detest.

"When all you have is hate and fear and loathing, it's hard to allow those you love inside those walls. I know that, but love is strong. Stronger thank you can ever imagine."

And so is betrayal.

Judas hit the button of his car key and lights flashed in the darkness. The more I cried, the more determined I was to turn the world upside down to help my father. He'd do the same for me.

"I'm scared," I murmured, more to myself, but it was loud enough for the guys to hear as they moved closer, arms around me, breath on my cheeks and neck.

"We're with you." Nero squeezed my hand. "And even though you might feel different right now, so is Judas."

I flinched with his words. Judas opened the passenger's side door and waited for me. Bond let go of my hand, and Nero followed. I held the Alpha's gaze as I slipped into his car and he closed the door. Muffled voices came from outside, both Nero and Bond climbed into the back seat without saying a word and a second later Judas was yanking open the driver's door and starting the car.

I curled in my seat and stared outside as Judas drove out of the Academy grounds, taking the corners too sharp.

Wheels skidded. I gripped the door to keep from slamming around in the seat and watched as we flew down darkened roads. "Where are we going?"

Judas didn't answer, just worked the gears and hugged the corners of the road as we drove south. I lost track of time, watching the moon and the way the car's headlights cut through the trees.

Until the car slowed and turned down a narrow dirt road. Fear slipped along my skin, catching my breath. I glanced to Judas. "Judas, where are we going?"

"To show you the truth," he answered. The muscles of his jaw bulged. "Maybe then you'll believe me."

The car bottomed out over dips and ridges, scraping the belly. We wound our way deeper through the dense trees and overgrowth. I reached out, stabbed the button for the window and cracked it open just a little. Cold, fresh air flooded the car. I inhaled, smelling the smoky tang of a fire, and the heady scent of the earth. But underneath that was something musky, something dangerous and animalistic—it was the scent of Wolves.

"This is your home...your pack." I wrenched my gaze to his.

A lone Vampire in the middle of a Wolf pack was a death sentence.

He cut me a glance, and those deep brown eyes stole me away. "We'll protect you. We'd never harm you."

"Trust us," Nero murmured from the back seat.

"We're here for you," Bond chimed in.

Judas swung the car around a hard bend and then slowed before he stopped. I searched the trees for movement and found none. A howl cut through the air as Judas shoved open his door and the others exited behind me. Maybe I should have asked Chuck and Ava to join me after all.

I caught the glow of a light through the trees. I could see it now, the faint dark outline of a towering mansion under the forest's shadow. The car doors boomed as they shut, in the absolute stillness of this place. Large windows shimmered against the moon light.

Four columns flanked two enormous black doors at the entrance, supporting a balcony on the first floor. But there was no life, no movement, so far removed from everything I knew.

"You live here?" I asked.

Judas rounded the hood of the car and reached out, asking me to take his hand. I hated that flinch of distrust inside me, still I reached out, took his hand in mine and let him lead me through the long grass toward the cold, empty house.

"I don't think anyone's home."

"Oh, they're home," Judas murmured, stepped over a fallen tree and kept on walking.

The snap of a twig to my right seized my gaze. Through the faint glow of the moon came the silver shine of eyes. Movement to my left made the skin on the nape of my neck crawl.

I could feel them now, all around me, closing in.

Every ravenous Wolf.

"I don't want to be here," I murmured and flinched at the low growl of an Alpha.

But Judas never gave me the option to turn and run, instead he mounted the steps of the old mansion and pulled me with him.

"You wanted to know the truth, and I'm showing you the truth. I want you to understand what lies ahead for your father. I want you to truly understand."

He slowed, letting me catch up, and then steered me along the verandah, toward a side door. I stumbled as I caught sight of the metal door, just like the one I'd seen in the dungeon at the Blood Moon Academy.

"What's inside there?"

He fiddled with a key and unlocked it, while I trembled, half of me toying with the idea of turning and running.

"You'll see." He palmed open the door and switched on a light.

Soft pale light spilled into the room. Judas stepped inside as an older woman pushed up from the rocking chair in the middle of the room. "Judas," she called.

He strode over to her, lowering his head and wrapped his arms around her soft body. "Is he...is he asleep?"

"Yes." She lifted her gaze and looked at me. Silver strands of her hair sparkled under the shine of the light, and the color was reflected in her eyes.

She was Wolf.

She was family.

"Nana, this is Morwenna."

"A Vampire," she growled as she patted his shoulder and met his gaze. "You bought a Vampire into my home?"

"She's a friend," he answered.

"Our friend, Nana," Nero added.

"And we are hers." Bond stepped closer.

"Her father has the sickness," Judas murmured. "She has to understand."

Sadness stole the silver shine of her eyes. The old woman just nodded. "Be careful,' she murmured to Judas. "Don't let him know it's you."

"I'll take her." Nero stepped closer.

But Judas shook his head. "No, this is my responsibility."

Worn floorboards howled and groaned as he headed along the hallway. But this time he didn't pull me after him, and the others didn't push at my back. They just waited, letting me make the decision to follow, or to flee.

I swallowed hard and walked the same path before he turned, opened what looked like the cellar door and stepped through. Heavy footsteps echoed. It was the Blood Moon Academy cells all over again. My stomach tightened as I strode down the steps to a heavy metal door on the cellar wall.

"In there," Judas murmured.

I glanced at him, and then the others behind me.

They waited. It was all on me.

Fear was a vice grip around my heart. I strode toward the door and gripped the handle. The locks Judas had removed had worn grooves into the door and the bolts. I glanced to the small table on my right and found the inch-thick clasps there waiting. There were four of them. Four to keep whatever was inside...in there.

"You can turn the light on," Judas spoke behind me. "He won't even know."

The door hinge was silent, greased and seamless, opening wide like the hungry jaws of a Wolf.

The stench hit me, foul and fetid, dripping with raw, animalistic hunger. My hand trembled as I reached inside, and felt along the doorframe and the wall for a light switch.

"Do not cry out," Judas whispered in my ear.

I flinched as the switch went *click,* and soft yellow light filled the space.

It took a moment for my mind to make sense of what I stared at. A man was slumped on the ground against the far wall of a cemented room. His head was down, arms wrapped around his knees. I stared at his hands, which were nothing more than mangled, malformed stumps. His chest rose and fell, the only movement that told me he was alive...if this was deemed living.

The man jerked his head upwards. Blackened, sunken holes filled the space where his eyes used to be. A cry ripped from my lips at the sight. I reached up and slapped a hand over my mouth as his nostrils flared and the ravenous, unmerciful sounds of something not quite right filled the space.

Judas was fast, throwing the switch, pulling me backwards before he yanked the door closed. Bond and Nero were there as a *boom* thundered against the inside of the door.

Locks slid into place and snapped shut as the steel vibrated from the blows. I stumbled backwards, imagining that *thing* slamming those broken, mangled stubs of hands against the surface.

"Who is that?" I cried out, revulsion clenching my belly. I swallowed again and again, stumbling away as acid spilled into my mouth.

I fell against the wall and sank to one knee, retching and sobbing. I couldn't stop seeing him, those hands...*those eyes.*

Acid spilled from my lips as that man slammed the inside of the door desperately. *Let him out!* I wanted to scream. *Let him out of there.* And all I could see was my father, my beautiful, sweet father in that cell in the Blood Moon Academy.

"Come on." Judas gripped under my arms and lifted.

He half carried me, helping me back up the stairs to the main house.

The scent of a fresh fire filled my nostrils as we walked back into the living room of the house. The old woman had lit a fire. Hungry amber tongues licked the bottom of an old kettle.

'Sit." She pointed to a worn sofa in the middle of the room.

The cellar door thudded closed behind us. Nero and Bond appeared a second later.

"I'll grab the mugs," Nero turned.

"I'll help you." Bond cut a glance to Judas and followed.

"Think maybe it's time you told your lady friend here the truth," his Grandmother cut me a glance. "I'm tired, and I'm going to bed. He'll be a handful tomorrow when the hunger kicks in. I'm going to need all my strength."

She reached out, gave him a soft pat on the top of the head before she leaned forward and kissed his cheek. He grasped her hand, pinning it to the side of his face, and murmured. "I love you."

This was such a different side of him, soft and comforting, meek for a powerful Alpha.

"Love you too, boy, take care at that fancy school now." Then she left, making her way to a flight of stairs that hugged the far wall. She climbed them slowly until she reached the first floor and then disappeared into the dark.

The fire crackled and snapped. Embers floated into the air as the water in the pot slowly boiled.

"Talk to me," I said, hating the silence of this place. I paused as my mind tried to catch up on everything I'd seen.

I never thought I'd crave the raucous laughter and loud clinks of champagne glasses, even the elegant drone of voices. But out here the quiet was almost painful.

"Do you see now?" He lifted his head. "Do you see what this curse does to you."

"W-who was that?" I asked.

His soft brown eyes darkened like cold, hard, grave dirt as he answered. "My father."

I gasped. "He's sick too?"

"It's a curse," he explained. "It started long ago with the Witches, but now it's spreading."

I struggled to make sense of his words, to stop my world from spinning. "What curse?"

"The curse that's haunted the Blackthorne family for centuries."

CHAPTER THREE

DARKNESS WAITS FOR YOU AT THE CROSSROADS

C*URSE*. T*HE* *WORD* *RACED* *THROUGH* *MY* *MIND*. "How...*why?* What does it want with my dad?"

Bond and Nero slipped into the room. One grabbed the handle of the kettle with a thick heavy mitt and poured water into the cups.

"No one knows why. The Witches have been trying to figure it out for centuries. What we can gather is this. It affects the strongest family lines first then slowly works its way out to the others."

Bond handed me a worn tin cup filled with steaming tea. Heat bled through cold skin, stinging the tips of my fingers. But I needed it. I needed warmth like I needed blood to survive. I wrapped my shaking hands around the metal tighter and dragged the rim to my lips.

"It changes them, Mor." Judas just held his tea and stared into the crackling fire. "It turns them into animals. The first time my dad attacked me we were out hunting. He just...snapped, slashed my stomach, tried to tear out my throat. If it wasn't for the others, I wouldn't have survived.

First, we thought it was poison, but then it happened again three days later, and that time he almost killed me."

My breath caught. His hand trembled around the mug. "You think I betrayed you at the dance, but I had to leave. I had to take the chance that Bond and Nero would protect you. You didn't see Keir walk in with the others, didn't see the terror written all over his face. Your father was headed for the dance, Morwenna. He was coming to kill you."

The cup slipped in my hand. My heart punched against my ribs as I shoved to stand. "No. No he wouldn't do that."

"And you think mine would? He raised me from a pup, even when my mother deserted me. He'd only ever been careful and kind, until that day. But that's the curse, it turns them against those they love the most."

"My mom?" I murmured.

"No, it seems to impact only their children, it's like some kind of force takes over. They don't understand what they're doing. You saw how my dad was. He tore out his own eyes to stop from seeing me, because in that moment he knew what he wanted to do. He thought if he can't see me, then he can't hurt me. It was the same with his hands, if he can't tear me, then maybe I can fight back. But now he just sits down there, and my grandmother takes care of him."

"Are you saying that's going to be my dad?"

He didn't say anything. Why didn't he say anything?

"It's just everything happening. The Diamonds, now this curse." My voice broke as a sob tore through me.

Hot tea splashed my hand. Nero lunged forward, catching the mug as it slipped. "Hey." Arms went around me. I couldn't see whose through the blur.

"It's not your fault. You weren't the one who used the Dragon's Tears as a way to kill and control. You weren't the one who planted that body in your room, and you aren't the one to blame now."

"But my dad is the one who is suffering, *you* are suffering too. And your dad, your poor dad."

"You don't need to think about that now. All you need to focus on is staying away from the Witch's Academy, and staying away from your dad." He leaned forward, reaching out to grasp my hand. "I'm not going to let anything happen to you, Morwenna. Trust me."

I swiped my tears with the back of my hand. I had trusted him, and then I'd felt betrayed. But he hadn't betrayed me at all. If anything, he'd stepped into danger to protect me. "Did my father...did he hurt you?"

"Let's just say he wasn't too keen on leaving the dance."

I curled my shoulders and turned away, not wanting him to see the pain in my face. All I could picture was my dad attacking Judas, and the image of that made my stomach churn. I'd been furious at Judas, and he'd been protecting me.

His hand gently touched my arm, curling over my bicep, and drawing me around to face him. "You don't need to hide from me. I know exactly what you're going through."

"Is there nothing we can do?"

He just shook his head. "They've tried every spell they know of. Tagar has even consulted with someone higher than him, but they can't break it."

Hopelessness consumed me. I was weighed down by the feeling, consumed by this desperate ache inside. I reached up, pressed my fingers against my chest as my heart gave a shudder. "No, I can't stand by. I can't just leave it to someone else. Not when his life is at stake...my dad."

"He's safe where he is for now. You want to search for this on your own?"

His brown eyes bored into mine, embers flickered in the darkness of those eyes, and for a second, I was consumed, swallowed by the endless night as he murmured, "Then we search together. We *figure it out* together."

Figure it out.

Figure out what the Witches couldn't...Witches far more powerful than us.

I swayed under the weight of it all, like a boulder the size of this damn house was crushing me. But through the mud and stone, and the jagged edges, love for my father cracked through, like the root of a tree, desperate to find purchase...desperate to hold on, and keep that mountain of dirt together.

Because that is how we'll survive.

By keeping it all together.

I turned to not just Judas, but to Nero and Bond. "I want to try. I want *us* to try. If you want to."

All three of my Wolves nodded. Nero rose at the same time as Bond. "We want to," both answered in unison.

"So, we start with Tagar," Judas stated. "We go back, figure this all out. We dig until we've unearthed every goddamn aspect of this curse. It's what I should've done a long time ago. But I was weak and afraid."

I was the one who reached for his hand this time. "You didn't have me then, but you do now."

Bond nodded, Nero just smiled. "I'll take these." He grabbed the mugs of tea that'd now gone cold.

Judas gave my hand a squeeze. "Come on, we still have to see the High Priest before we get back to school."

I let him lead me out of the old house and onto the verandah. Silver eyes waited for me as I looked around the darkened forest. They crowded the trees, some standing upright in their human form, others stayed as Wolves on all fours. Judas gave a nod and led me down the stairs as Nero and Bond followed, switching off the light and plunging us into darkness. But I didn't need the light, not anymore.

I felt them more than saw them. Their desperation, their sadness.

This curse affected more than Judas and me. It affected an entire pack.

The mysterious Blackthorne Wolves weren't really mysterious at all. They were desperate and cautious, they didn't like outsiders, most of all ones like me, and as that thought filled me, so did the flare of determination.

I'd find this curse.

I'd tear it out by the roots.

I'd stop this from happening to any other family.

We strode through the forest working our way back to the car, leaving the Blackthorne secrets behind. A car door thudded in the quiet night. Judas started the engine and pulled the car around, driving us out the way we'd come.

I had a lot to think about on the drive back to Blood Moon Academy. So many questions swirled around inside my head, but the one which took up the most space was about to be answered. The diamonds weren't really diamonds. They were Dragon's tears, a powerful tool used as a vessel to capture power.

The Demons used these tears to take power from the Ancient, Vlad Vasile, and that filtered down through all the Vampires in his coven, including my family, but somehow I wasn't affected. Not like everyone else. I was protected by the woman in black.

The Demons almost killed my family and my friends, and all for of power and control. They wanted to force those left behind back into the shadows, so they could reign supreme.

Judas turned the wheel as we hit the asphalt, heading to the Blood Moon Coven for the second time tonight. They didn't want me there, didn't want me to trigger this *need* in my father to hurt me, but they had answers...and I had questions.

I pressed my spine against the seat, taking in the quiet sound of the car and feeling of strength around me until the haunting, crimson glow of the Coven's windows glowed in the night.

"How long have you known them?" I turned to Judas.

"The Witches, you mean?"

"Yeah."

"Tagar came to our door the day my father first attacked me. He took my grandmother aside, spoke to her in hushed tones. I was angry, frightened, not much more than a boy, trying to be a man. She cried, talking to the Warlock. That sight stayed with me. I'd never seen her as anything but strong. Tagar has been back many times, trying one spell or another. He managed to slow the spread of the curse in the hopes we might figure this out. It took all his power to do just that." He pulled the car into the parking lot and switched off the engine before turning to me. "Wait here, I'll be back."

And he was gone, heading for the front door of the Academy.

"Don't be afraid of Tagar," Nero murmured. "He looks intimidating."

"Acts like it too," Bond snarled.

"Just, whatever you do, don't let him know you're afraid of him." Nero murmured. "He'll use that against you."

A tremor cut through me. I tried to still the unease. If anything, I should be grateful. Tagar had tried to help me. Even though I didn't know him at all.

Movement came from the front door of the Academy. Judas sprinted toward us and slowed before yanking open the driver's door and climbing in. "He's not coming."

"What do you mean he's not coming?" I cut a glare toward the towering building and clenched my jaw as I reached for the clasp of the seatbelt.

But Judas shook his head. "He wants us to meet him somewhere."

I stilled. "Where?"

"At the crossroads."

Crossroads? "What crossroads?"

"The only one that matters," Judas murmured and started the car.

He backed out, and then shot forward, turning left instead of right. The outskirts of Tricks City was a mangle of bright lights and darkened corners. A few smatterings of eclectic furniture shops mingled with the Spend-Less Grocery shops and Liquor stores. But we went near none of those.

Instead Judas drove behind the built up streets to the middle of nowhere, where the city was far behind us and only fields surrounded us. Or it felt like it at least. He pulled the car up on the edge of the road and killed the engine. Long grass hugged the edges of the tarmac on all corners. One towering streetlight splashed white light on the asphalt.

It was a crossroad.

An actual crossroad.

I cracked open my door and climbed out. The light bulb buzzed and flickered above me, insects plunged into the glare only to fall to the ground, unmoving.

Doors opened and closed as the Wolves got out. The

sound echoing in the night. "I guess we just wait," I murmured.

"Not for long." Judas nodded toward a lone dark figure striding toward us.

And Tagar Lutherian, the High Priest of the Blood Moon Coven lifted his gaze and stepped under the pale light.

CHAPTER FOUR

THERE'S NO GUARANTEES WHEN DEALING WITH THE DEVIL

THE SNARL OF A WOLF ECHOED IN THE NIGHT, whipping around me as the cool night breeze seemed to suddenly change, bringing with it a bitter chill.

I shivered, watching Tagar stride closer, dressed in leather.

"Can you feel it?" The High Priest lifted his gaze to mine. "Witching hour is upon us."

A shudder slipped along my spine as I watched him. Tagar was younger than I'd expected, tall and incredibly handsome, with the kind of angsty blue-green eyes that pinned you in place. I tried to read him, tried to understand him.

"This place is steeped in power. No one goes unscathed from a deal at the crossroads."

What did that actually mean?

"All I feel is the freezing cold," Nero muttered behind me.

Judas was at my back, his hands rubbing the chill out of my arms, and I leaned into his touch.

"Why are we here?" I asked the Warlock as I drew Judas' arms around me.

Tagar strolled toward the middle of the crossroad and waved me over. "Only you," he demanded. "Come."

Judas' hand went around my wrist, holding me in place for a second, and then released.

I steeled myself, took a breath and then strode forward. I'd face the Devil himself if it meant I could save my dad.

I closed the distance, leaving the Wolves for the buzzing of insects and the long dark road. Silence found me, like a vacuum, as I stepped right into the middle.

"If quiet long enough, you'll hear the Demons at the Gates of Hell offering to make you a deal." He smirked. Shadows danced across his face, his eyes were wide and seemed to brighten, his body seeming to grow larger. He was enjoying this darkness, flirting with danger.

"I'm fine, thanks. The only deal I want is the one where my father is not chained up in your basement."

He just gave a slow smile and nodded.

"What's so special about this place anyway?" I asked, then glanced over my shoulder at my three Wolves, standing beneath the street light, hands in their pockets, but their gazes were trained on me. Ready to leap should anything go wrong. Having them so close eased my nerves.

"There was no saving the Blackthorne line," he started. "I tried, believe me, I tried. I dug through thousands of ancient texts, scoured every Witch from Tricks City all the way to the state line. I even approached the Nightcomers, and not even those Witches knew what caused it, or had a cure. Whatever this is, it's powerful, and dark. So, when your father first came to me I turned to the only thing left. The Mother of Night. I came to this place with the Tears, intending to use them against the curse."

"The Tears? You mean the Dragon Tears? It was you...you made us sick?"

"No, not entirely. They were stolen," he met my gaze, and searched my eyes. "But whoever took them had no idea the Tears already contained power I intended to use. I didn't know they were gone until your father contacted me about the curse."

I shook my head. "It wasn't just the blood sickness though, was it?"

"No."

"Dante knew the moment he found the mark. He knew the curse was finding his way to your line. It's what bought him to me in the first place." He stared down the long, lonely road as though he couldn't bear to look at me. "But now any hope of breaking the curse is gone, along with the Tears."

"Can't you just find more?"

He turned to me then, and murmured. "There *are* no more. They were it, the only ones in existence. The only thing powerful enough to contain even a fraction of Hekate's power. With that fraction, I might've stood a chance. But not now."

"And this Hekate can't help you any other way?" I asked as an icy chill slipped across my skin.

"No, she can't. Hekate is more than a Witch. She's a goddess of magic, witchcraft, and necromancy. She's the goddess of crossroads, of necromancy and ghosts...and the night. I summoned her once, and she doesn't take kindly to that."

He yanked his shirt open. A savage, deep gash started just under his collarbone, and reached deeper. Crusted edges were starting to heal, still it looked red, hot and painful. "Payment for tapping into her energy. I got off lightly."

Someone cleared their throat and I glanced over to the Wolves, who watched the Warlock without a word.

And the chill in the air moved deeper, plunging into my bones. I shuddered, ground my jaw to still the chatter of my teeth and glanced toward the edge of the field.

She stood there, the woman in black, watching...*waiting*.

"What does she look like?" I murmured. "Hekate."

"It depends. She's the triple Goddess; maiden, mother, crone. She comes to you in the face of someone you need."

"Shrouded in black, distant, powerful, has a pentacle carved into her palm?"

Tagar stilled, and then turned his gaze toward me, eyes widening. "You saw her?"

"Still see her actually," I murmured and nodded to the edge of the road, where she waited amongst the grass.

He followed my gaze, but I could tell that he didn't see her. Not like I did. "Interesting that she comes to you so easily, while I spent two months of nights calling for her. Has she asked something of you? Given you a gift?"

"No, she's just been there." *Hekate.*

The name rolled through my mind. I wanted to know more about her. Who she was, why she haunted me, and what it meant for her now the Dragon Tears were gone.

Energy buzzed in my ear. The sound growing louder as the streetlight brightened. Something smacked into my face. The buzz of an insect followed. I swatted the damn thing and whipped my head right and left.

It felt like a thousand of them crawled along my arms, until a loud *bang* echoed above.

Sparks exploded in every direction like fireworks, and

then a blanket of darkness fell over us, bleeding into the shadows.

I jerked my gaze toward the tall grass where she stood as footsteps closed in behind me. The Wolves were there in seconds. Their hands sliding along my arm, chasing that crawling feeling away.

"You okay?" Judas growled, the deep sound washed over me.

Bond's hand rested on my back. Nero stood in front of me.

And in their presence I felt invincible.

A spark of light illuminated from the Warlock's hand. The bitter stench of sulphur filled the air. I knew that smell, and knew what came from it. The flicker of light grew bolder, driving through the darkness like a mighty swing from a bat. Faces rushed forward from the gloom, deformed, twisted, demonic faces with hellish-red eyes, foul blackened teeth on show.

"Fucks sake!" Bond snarled.

"Get to your car!" Tagar roared.

My feet left the ground, someone grabbed me and heaved me over their shoulder. I had no time to see before I was jolted and jostled, heavy thudding steps filled my head as insects swarmed us around us.

Car doors were opened, and I was thrown across the backseat before a muscled body piled on top.

"Sorry," Bond murmured, his warm breath skimming my cheek.

I dug my heel into the seat, scooting backwards as Nero pushed in. Hands gripped me, fingers skimmed my legs, searching.

"Did they bite you?" Bond growled, rough hands,

roamed over my thigh, turning me, reaching for the strands of hair across my face.

"No, no I'm okay," I answered.

But I could smell blood. *Wolf Blood.*

The driver's door was thrown open, and Judas climbed in as I searched Bond's eyes under the interior lights. "You're hurt."

Nero yanked open the passenger's door and climbed in. I pushed upwards, pressing my back against the door as an inhuman scream cut through the air from somewhere outside. Tagar Lutherian yanked open the rear door, scanned the Wolves before stilling on me. "Let me know if she comes to you again. Hurry now, leave this place." Before he turned and took off.

He was a blur of black in the darkness, lunging through the tall grass. I caught the shift of movement somewhere to his right, and knew she was out there watching.

This Witch Goddess.

Hekate.

I climbed inside, slammed the door behind me before turning to Bond "Let me see."

Judas started the car and we were moving, swinging wide before accelerating hard the way we'd come, but I couldn't look at the beasts out there hunting us. All I could see was the bloodied slash on Bond's shoulder, deep, flowing freely. My stomach clenched as the past returned. I knew exactly what Wolf blood would do to a Vampire, and my body shuddered in warning.

"It's okay," he murmured, green eyes growing darker. "I heal fast."

"No." I slid a hand under his arm and pulled him closer against me. "Let me stem the flow."

I pressed my hand against the wound, feeling him stiffen.

Pain made him catch his breath and wince. Still I pressed tighter, forcing the torrent to well inside the gash, then I leaned closer and kissed him.

He stiffened, lips barely moved, the chaste kiss turned hungry as I parted my lips. A tremor cut through his body, and he seemed to melt against me. Hungry lips widened, taking more. He braced his body against the seat beside me and drove me backwards.

Still I never let go of the wound, using every ounce of strength to stem the flow.

He was bigger than Judas, his thick, heavy chest pressed against mine. Lips taking a little more as he lifted his hand and slid a calloused thumb down my cheek.

Desire welled in his eyes as he eased away, breaking the kiss. The twitch of a smile, set my nerves on fire as he murmured, "I think I'm good now."

"Yeah, we think he's good too," Nero snarled, blue eyes sparkling with a hint of jealousy.

I glanced at Judas who just eyed his Beta and then gave a chuckle. "You look fucking proud of yourself."

Bond just laughed. "Yep, bitten and kissed almost at the same time." He leaned back and then winced as my hand slipped free. "Ow, that fucking hurts."

"I'm sorry." I cringed.

"That place gives me the creeps." Nero stared out of the window.

I searched for the High Priest, tearing my gaze to Judas. "Maybe we should have offered the High Priest a lift to the Blood Moon Academy?"

"Don't think he would've accepted," Judas muttered. "Heard he can turn into mist and just...vanish."

"No way, really?" I murmured.

"Well, he's the only Witch I'd ever heard of who could summon Hekate and still live. I'd say he's got a hell of a lot of magic mojo," Nero turned toward me. "I'm sure he can take care of himself."

The car growled as we sped back to school. But Nero's words stayed with me all the way back to the Academy grounds.

I woke with the sun glaring through my blinds and turned over. Everything seemed so still, so calm, so safe, so different. Yesterday had been the shittiest day of my life, but I had answers...

Well, some answers at least. Others remained a mystery, much like the woman in black on the side of the road.

Dad would insist I keep studying, keep trying, keep upholding the Livingstone name. When all I wanted to do was to leave this place, to go home and take care of Mom. But that wouldn't solve anything, would it?

I climbed out of bed to get ready for the day. By the time I was done, sleep had been long forgotten so I headed out of my room, just as Chuck backed out of Ava's, gently pulling the door closed without making a sound.

I smirked, leaned against the wall, and waited.

When he finally lifted his head, he flinched, and snorted a fake laugh. "What are you doing?"

"What are *you* doing?" I pushed off the wall, clucking my tongue. "You're not allowed in students' dorms."

"Ava asked for my help."

"Sure she did." I loved teasing him, yet he stood there

tall and proud, pulling down on his tee, acting like he'd done nothing wrong.

"I was outside your room most of the night after I saw you return with the Wolves. But earlier this morning, Ava came running to me about a huge spider in her room." The corners of his mouth twitched as if he fought to hold a straight, honest face.

And I couldn't hold it back anymore, I burst out laughing, clasping my stomach. "Thank you for making me laugh. I needed this so much." Tears collected in my eyes from chuckling.

He stared at me with a strange look. "You've got this wrong."

"No, I don't," I snapped back. I knew a guilty face when I saw one.

A sudden, sharp scream erupted from Ava's room, and I shuddered.

Chuck turned and pushed open her door. I bolted after him.

Ava was standing on top of her desk in her school pleated skirt and white shirt, holding a broom with both hands, pointing it to a swarm of black insects crawling over her ceiling from a crack in the corner.

"What the hell!" I yelled.

"Fucking spider sack. I poked it and must have burst it open. Get the damn bug spray. Get ten of them. We're gonna spray them out of existence."

"No need to kill them," Chuck insisted. "Let me collect them and take them outside."

"Are you insane?" Ava blurted. "They'll be back, then they'll be pissed and crawl into my ears while I sleep. Kill them! Better yet, *burn the whole fucking place to the ground!*"

"You two go to class," Chuck mumbled. "I'll take care of this." He gripped Ava's waist and picked her up off the table and placed her on the floor before taking the broom from her grip.

He turned to me and gave me a satisfied grin, the kind that said, *told you so.*

"Oh, just shut up!" I whirled on my heels, grabbed Ava by the arm, and dragged her outside her room.

Maybe I didn't know a guilty face after all.

CHAPTER FIVE

HELLHOUNDS ARE JUST PLAIN HELL

Classes were weird. I jumped at every sound, forced every laugh, constantly glancing at the doorway expecting another horde of Demons to come rushing through,

"Hey, you okay?" Ava murmured, following my gaze to the doorway.

I smiled, nodded, and then kept scribbling down the page numbers on the board.

"Pop Quiz tomorrow people," Mr. Gomez called out.

The entire class groaned as the bell rang out. Chairs were shoved backwards as students sprinted for the doorway.

"You got a class with Leathers?" Ava hung back, eyeing the massive Understudy book.

"Yep," I sucked in a hard breath and sighed. This whole charade was useless. I didn't want to be here. I wanted to be hunting down whatever information I could find about the damn curse.

While I was here, playing 'student' my father was chained in a cell in the Blood Moon Academy's cellar.

"I can skip tortuous translations and come with you, if you want?" she suggested. "Sounds boring anyway."

I chuckled and shook my head. "And risk the wrath of Ms. Servitude?" I muttered, wincing at the new teacher's name.

I grabbed the Understudy's Bible, heaved it to balance against my hip and strode toward the door. There was a blackened mark on the doorway. The touch of a hand that singed the wood. The influx of new teachers hadn't been the only thing that'd changed after the Demon attack.

I glanced along the hallway to where the Principal's office stood. Principal Stone's name had already been removed. The rumor was that she'd left in the wake of the attack by her own kind, driven away by terror or humiliation.

But I knew better.

Principal Stone was pushing up daisies for lack of a better description. She hadn't run off. She'd outright attacked me, forcing me to defend myself. But she was gone...and we now had a new Principal.

Burn marks were etched into the walls. Metal door handles had melted, and then hardened in some twisted macabre monstrosity.

"Move along," the snarl came at my right as I stood in the middle of the hallway.

"You *move along*," Ava snapped back.

I reached out, grabbed her arm and pushed her forward. The new Principal had bought his own guards with him, and they were everywhere. The hallways. The dorms. Hell, four of them glared at us from the cafeteria.

I glanced over my shoulder at the glowing red eyes from the guard and winced.

The Academy had changed, and it wasn't for the better.

The foul stench of burning sulphur wafted down the hall.

"Fine, see you after class," Ava murmured and turned away.

The air trembled with hostility. Hellhounds brought with them their own version of Hell. And this was mine, being watched at every corner, being *expected* to have it all together. Everyone knew I was to blame for the attack, and everyone knew the Vampire line was weak.

And when an immortal line was weak, they were subject to attack. The door opened to the Principal's office and Balefire, the Hellhound stepped out.

The air seemed to grow warmer as he turned his head and glared my way. I glanced at the floor and hurried past, feeling his annoyance like the heat of a fire. I glanced over my shoulder as I turned the corner. He was still watching me, still *hating me*. Principal Balefire.

I stilled at the classroom for the Understudy lessons and grabbed the door handle. It was one of the few that wasn't malformed and melted. Strange. I yanked open the door and stepped inside. "Mr. Leathers?"

There wasn't an answer, not at first, and then a low, snappy growl. "You're late."

I came around the edge of the walkway and stared. Nefarious had rearranged the seats so that they faced the rear of the classroom...which was now the front. I pointed to the seats, and then to the desk where he sat. "Done some redecorating, huh?"

"Sit down, Morwenna, and we can start."

Oh, *okay*...I neared the desk at the front of the class-room. Every class I'd had with him had been more of an informal discussion on my role as an Understudy...*until now.*

He'd changed too. Gone were the see-through black mesh shirts and leather. He wore a long sleeved button up shirt...that was buttoned-up, all the way to his neck. Black trousers fell neatly, not hugging like the leather used to do as he stood and moved around the desk.

"I'm not here to be your friend," he started, eyes downcast, not even bothering to look at me as I slid into a seat and dropped the massive book to the table. "I'm here to teach, and to inform you that your role of the Understudy isn't just a title. You don't get to play house and not clean the damn house."

"Oh, wow. Where the Hell is this coming from Mr. Leathers? 'Cause the last time we saw each other you were kinda grateful to be alive."

"Grateful? Relieved more like it," he answered. "Things have changed Morwenna."

"No shit."

He cut me a glare, and then a second later it softened. Then he glanced toward the doorway at the back of the classroom...the front now, actually. Fuck, I don't know. It was the second damn class for the day and already I was confused.

"The time for discussion is over, now you have to act...walk the talk, so to speak, or *whatever*." He reached behind him for some ugly ass, yellow covered book that I was sure had been white...*once,* and handed it to me. "This is the previous Understudy's journal. Read it, understand it. Do it."

Oh Hell, I was not touching that thing. "Um, that was when, exactly?" I lifted my gaze to his. "Because things have changed in the last century...or ten."

He looked at the brittle, small thing in his hand and stilled. "Yes, I guess you're right. But the fact is that blood supply is at an all time low, and after the wave of sickness, mortals are running scared."

"Scared of what?"

Dark eyes glinted. "The same thing they're always scared of. Us."

"There hasn't been a mortal attack in ages," I muttered and shook my head.

He turned and cast the book onto his desk. "Try telling them that. It is your job, and the Ancient sent his courier to my room early this morning. Vlad is frail. He refuses to come out of his room. So, the instruction was to instruct you. Do your job, Understudy. Get the blood supply back to those who need it the most."

He stepped around to his desk and yanked out his chair then slipped quietly into the seat and picked up a pen.

Was that it? I waited, nervously looking from him to the empty room. "I can't do this alone."

"You're not alone. I'm here and you have my number, so call me if you need. But I need to see how you'll perform. Now, take a seat and let's go through what you'll expect."

I nodded and despite the unease in my stomach, I was ready to find out how I could help as part of my Understudy role.

An hour later, I rose from my chair and grabbed my Understudy Bible and eyed the journal one last time before I turned and walked out.

The door closed behind me with a *thud,* and the echo slipped down the hall.

Do your job, Understudy. He kept repeating during the study.

The words were ravenous, consuming space in my head. Everyone else was still in class. I walked along the empty hallway, steps slow...mind a million miles away.

Panicked thoughts crept in. I was the Understudy. I was the one to fix it all. He'd be there for me he insisted, but I was still the one to take the lead. What if I failed?

A low snarl came from beside me. "You should be in class."

I jerked my gaze up to the Hellhound guard standing sentry outside the Principal's office. "Free period," I muttered and kept on walking, all the way along the hallway to the door outside.

The warm sun beat down, but I barely felt the rays. All I felt was a growing sense of unrest, tangled with hopelessness. I walked until I forgot I was walking. The diamonds. My Dad. The curse...and now...*Witches*. A High Priest to be exact. Plus, there were the demons and the woman in black. It hurt my head to keep track of them all.

I lifted my head when I reached the corner of a building, but it wasn't my dorm. I glanced behind me and then rounded the corner and walked to the front of the building. I'd taken the long way around the Academy grounds and ended up...here.

The front door of the small cottage opened, and a towering male filled the doorway. But this time there was no snarl of a command, this time there was a small smile. "Morwenna, everything okay?" Chuck took a step toward me.

"Yes...no. I don't know."

His brow furrowed as he scanned the bushes behind me. I wanted to sink myself into the memory of this morning, just for a second...just until the happiness returned. But I couldn't, not now.

"Want to come in and we'll talk about it?"

He'd always been just like a father to me, always protecting, always...*there*. I nodded and followed him inside. The faintly sour smell of fetid blood still lingered, no matter how many times he'd scrubbed the place from floor to ceiling. Or maybe it was just me. Maybe I was the one trapped in the past, unable to move forward.

"Want some blood?"

I shook my head and turned. "Who am I?"

He waited for a second, unsure. "Morwenna Livingstone."

"No, I mean...*who am I?*"

He was silent, watching.

"Am I a daughter, or an Understudy?" I threw my hand in the air. "I don't even know who I am, should've stayed at home, should've never come to this place."

"You know you don't mean that. Sit, talk to me, tell me what I can do."

"There's nothing you *can* do." I strode into the living room and flopped onto the sofa. "Dad's chained up, there's some kind of curse that's now going to turn him into a rabid animal bent on killing me, that I somehow accelerated when a pack of Demons tried to take some damn magical diamonds and force us into the darkness. Now...now I'm supposed to push all that aside and meet with the mortals to get them to send blood. I can't do this, Chuck. I can't be all this to everyone. I'm one hundred years old, how am I supposed to know anything at this age?"

"Who are you?" He turned my own question on me. "Look at me."

I met his cold, unflinching stare and shuddered.

"Who are you, Morwenna? Tell me."

"I...ah, I don't know."

"Yes, you do. Tell me the first thing people see when they look at you?"

"My father."

There was a nod of his head. "You have every one of his

traits, the good...and the bad. You're strong, fiercely loyal. You've made friends at this school, and your share of enemies. But you are one thousand percent you. You've never shied from a fight, even when that fight isn't yours to begin with. You can't blame yourself for your dad. All you can do is honor him. Be the young woman he knows you to be. Be that fire, be that obnoxious pain in the ass."

I cocked my head at him.

"Be you. Be Morwenna Livingstone."

"They want me to have a meeting with the mortals. I don't know how."

"Easy," he murmured. "It's just like every other party. Dress the part, smile, act like the Livingstone you are." He strode towards me and held out his hand.

I reached up, taking his grasp just like I'd done a thousand times before.

"Make them respect you," he murmured and seized my gaze with the look of a predator. "And if that doesn't work, I'll make sure they fear you."

"You're going to do *what?*" Ava was riveted as I told her.

"You know, you don't have to look so goddamn...*excited.*"

"I can see it now." She swept her hand through the air. Morwenna Livingstone, daughter of the infamous Dante Livingstone, protected by her bodyguards, Ava and Chuck."

"You are not my bodyguard."

But there was no stopping her. She just grinned like an idiot and smiled. "I can do it." She shoved up from the bed.

Held her hands up, smiled and then gave me a creepy-ass wink.

In an instant, tentacles unfurled from her body, two peeked out from under her skirt, three or four more from her shirt. I gave up counting...and looking, as she started to sing.

"You are not singing the Bodyguard soundtrack by Whitney Houston, are you?"

"*I will protect you with my life!*" she cried out.

I flopped back onto the bed and stared at the ceiling. "This is going to be a total nightmare."

She stilled. I saw the tip of a tentacle creeping toward me, before the slick end touched my nose. "*Boop!*"

"Ava," I warned.

"Okay, no bodyguard." She sulked and sat at the end of my bed. But only for a damn second before she lifted her head and those blue eyes sparkled with something I knew was just going to make me roll my eyes. "But I can be your assistant."

I opened my mouth as she slid from the bed, onto her knees. "Please, Morwenna. *Please.* Every Drug Lord needs a second, someone they can bark orders too. Someone who hands them the shot glass of whiskey. *I can be that second.*"

"I'm not a Drug Lord, and you need to stop watching Ozarks." I muttered.

But she just stared, fluttering her lashes...wearing me the Hell down.

And I caved. I closed my eyes and sighed. "Please don't embarrass me."

Sparkling white teeth were all I saw when I lifted my head and saw her grin.

CHAPTER SIX

SWEATING LIKE A BEAST

Ava kept fidgeting, crossing and recrossing her legs in the limousine. She'd changed from her warrior outfit into one that screamed librarian, with her pencil tight skirt falling to her knees, a wide collared pink shirt, and her hair pulled into a bun on top of her head, complete with a pencil threaded through it. Granted, she looked cute, but she belonged in the eighties with that style.

"If you're going for the Basic Instinct look, you're doing a great job," I murmured.

Chuck cleared his throat loudly from the driver's seat. God, maybe these two just needed to finally kiss and get it over with.

Ava leaned back, reaching a hand for Chuck. "Don't worry my teddy bear, it's all for you."

I laughed as I watched him roll his eyes, then he proceeded to shut the glass window between our compartment and his.

"Why are the windows so dark?" Ava leaned over and ran a hand over the super tinted windows as if that would make a difference.

"We're Vampires remember, and Dad wanted a limo in case we didn't have our rings."

Just thinking of Dad reminded me of what I was doing... Me, the Master Vamp's daughter about to attend a meeting with the spokesman for the humans when I couldn't even stand in front of the class without sweating like a beast.

Ava slouched in her seat and pulled on the fabric of her black skirt. "How do people walk in these things, and if I need to pee, you may need to cut me out of it."

"You'll be fine once we get out of the limo." Yet I couldn't stop my knees from bouncing. All the reasons I would fail came rushing through me as if my brain was setting me up for it. And that soft thread of panic started in the pit of my stomach, weaving and spreading, growing into a vortex. I gasped for air even though I didn't need oxygen.

"You okay, babe?" Ava asked.

I shook my head. "Y-yeah."

She cocked her head sideways and shuffled forward, placing her hand on my thigh. "Stop stressing. You'll do amazing. All you have to do is tell them everything is under control and to start sending Vamps blood again, and if that doesn't work, I'll just eat one. That should do the trick."

I snorted a response. "As if it were that simple. This is serious. What if I get stage fright? I might freeze like those people who are camera shy, and I'll sweat nonstop and probably drool in front of everyone. They'll have cameras, and oh hell. I can't do this." I was shaking my head again. What was I thinking, accepting this mission? Damn Mr. Leathers for forcing me into this situation, just because he was angry. Well, we were all having a shitty week.

Ava came over to my seat and sat next to me, her hand covering mine. "I'd tell you take a deep breath but not sure it would help. So just think of the end result. How you'll blow them away. Pretend you're talking to me when you present, to help you relax."

"This must be why they say to picture everyone naked."

"If it's your thing, go for it, but I wouldn't, especially if the room ends up being filled with stuffy, old, balding men in suits."

I chuckled and was grossed out at the same time at the image she painted. For the rest of the ride, we sat hand in hand, and I kept reminding myself this would become part of my new job as an Understudy. I'd have to get used to this, and I'd watched Dad lead such meetings. He had everyone eating out of his hand with his charisma. So that was all I needed.

"Maybe I should start the meeting with a joke?"

Ava cut me a sharp stare. "Not sure that's a good idea. Your jokes suck. I say go with the direct approach."

"Okay, okay, I can do that. I say my piece and walk out."

We came to a stop and the engine switched off. The moment the back door opened, Chuck offered me his hand. My stomach churned as if butterflies were in my gut, or maybe a goddamn butterfly war was going on in there.

"Morwenna," he hissed through clenched teeth.

With a nudge from Ava, I accepted his hand and climbed out of the car to be greeted by an avalanche of paparazzi and people crowding the footpath.

Next, Ava slid out of the car, legs first like a snake, and Chuck hoisted her to her feet.

Cameras flashed from the reporters, Ava was stunned for a second before I grabbed her hand and pulled her with us. Then we all rushed past the flashing cameras, the voices calling my name, asking where my dad was, but I kept my head low.

I didn't want to answer any of those questions.

Not now.

Instead, I followed Chuck into the building, avoiding everyone's stares. He stopped at a bank of elevators, hit the button and we waited. It felt like forever with the reporters screaming at us for an 'exclusive'.

Finally, the light came to life over the door and the elevator opened. We were moving, climbing each floor. I adjusted my clothes for the hundredth time before we stopped and the doors opened.

A woman nodded at us. "Ms. Livingstone, this way." And escorted us into some kind of boring boardroom.

The room was massive. Stretching out to the size of three or four conference rooms I'd seen before. Those who were waiting stared at us, like we were monsters.

To them, we probably were.

"This way," Chuck urged, his hand went to the small of my back, reassuring me.

I glanced at Ava.

She gave a nod, mouthing the words, *you got this*.

But I didn't. This was one of those times when everyone believed in me, and any second now they'd all discover I was a huge fake, pretending to be something I wasn't.

"Not sure about this. What if when I try to speak only garbage comes out?"

Mr. Leather's words settled over my mind. *Do your job, Understudy.* It reminded me I was tasked with this, no matter how much I shook.

Chuck looked down at me and smiled. "You're a Living-stone. Everyone fears your family, so you have nothing to worry about."

"Now show them how much you rock." Ava reached over and pinched my cheeks.

"Ouch." I batted her hands away.

"Trying to add a little color."

Chuck took my elbow. "It's time. You only need to make a statement. A request."

I swallowed the lump in my throat and waved to Ava before pushing one leg after the other, through the door Chuck opened. My stomach dropped as I looked at the rows of chairs, each one filled. So many people. Mostly men. Suits. Not a smile in sight.

Yep, this was the big league where adults played, and I felt like a bug under a microscope.

Chuck directed me to the table across the front, facing what felt like the inquisition.

Everything blurred together as my nerves jumbled under my skin, and I fumbled with a chair before sitting down, thankful to be off my shaky legs.

The spokesman, a man in his mid-fifties, approached me, all open-mouthed grin, his peppered hair slicked back from his face. Dressed in a pristine suit, he greeted me with a handshake then drew me to my feet and pulled me into a hug. I'd seen him in many meetings with Dad, who didn't think highly of the man, but said he was innocent enough for a human.

"I'm so sorry to hear about your father," he whispered in my ear, his voice sounding sincere. But beneath his voice, I heard the thudding of his heart, inhaled his perspiration. He was nervous... or was that fear?

Then he broke free and drew me to a pedestal with a microphone stand.

Okay, I wasn't meant to sit down; my cheeks were on fire. When I climbed up, I stared out over the packed room, searching for familiar eyes and found Ava and Chuck a few rows down, sitting on the edge. They both smiled, and it eased me somewhat.

"Morwenna, come closer, child," the spokesman murmured, waving me up to the microphone. He adjusted the stand to reach me, and yet something about the way he said, child, loud enough for others to hear, made me feel insignificant and small in a room full of people who probably hated vampires. And here I was, a kid, about to make a request.

So many emotions fluttered through me, and my gaze kept sweeping over the eyes staring at me, judging me. I'd worn my power suit—Gucci pants and soft curved jacket with a lace number underneath. Just enough softness to show I had sympathy.

Though right now it was glued to me from sweat.

As I stepped forward, the back door opened and my three Wolves slipped in, standing at the back of the room without anyone knowing.

A surge of energy burst through me at the sight.

They were here, protecting me, supporting me. I wasn't alone. I had those who loved me by my side.

I lifted my chin and grabbed the microphone, wrenching it out of the mic stand, which then lurched sideways.

The spokesman lunged for it, snatching it before it fell and I raised the microphone to my lips, wondering how they'd react if I broke into a song. Yep, one quick way to make Dad furious when he found out.

Instead, I cleared my throat and brought to mind the speech I'd practiced.

"Hello." My voice boomed through the speakers, the feedback squealed and everyone cringed, except for Ava, who giggled, gaining herself a glare from a young woman in pearls. I loved the sound of her chuckles.

I lowered the mic slightly and began again. "Hello, I'm

Morwenna Livingstone, and today I stand before you in place of my father. I understand that there are some concerns over the recent sickness that swept through Ancient Vlad Vasile and subsequently, the entire Vampire Brood, but I'm here to assure you that the illness was short lived, and apart from a low supply from your blood banks, we are back to normal." I rushed the words and a drop of sweat rolled down my spine, but I hadn't stumbled yet. Yay me.

A middle-aged man in a police suit, most likely the commissioner, shot his hand up, but spoke as if that gave him the okay to start speaking. "What about the attacks? The Precinct has been inundated with calls for help from people being attacked by your kind?"

My kind?

Others in the audience broken into chatter, others raised their hands, and I heard the words, *attacks, rampage, wild.* They were scared, all of them.

More hands shot up, more claims of attacks.

The commissioner was on his feet and approaching the front of the room. Chuck was at my side in a flash, standing tall like a soldier, guarding me. But the officer pushed a small handful of black and white photos of dead mortals toward me, and I studied each one, the gruesome bodies, their throats torn out and bloody.

"What are *you* going to do about these?" he barked.

I lifted my gaze to meet the Commissioner, facing the disgust behind his gaze, and I handed him the photos, not flinching, not giving him the emotional reaction he expected.

Instead I dug deep and drew on the strength inside me, just as Dad had shown me.

"I didn't know about this. I promise you. I'll personally

make sure these cases are investigated, and those respon-sible will be held accountable. I give you my word, and the word of a Livingstone is a guarantee." Dad's own words echoed in my head.

The Commissioner's upper lip curled. He didn't believe me. He sure as Hell didn't see me as an Understudy. I cringed from the distrust and looked around the room.

I was just a child to them.

Just a child playing dress-up.

The Commissioner turned away from me, shaking his head as he headed toward the exit.

I raised the microphone to my mouth. "You may wonder what authority I have to stand here and tell you that all will be well. I'm not just a Livingstone, daughter of a Master Vampire, but Understudy to the Ancient Vlad Vasile, and it is my task to govern the laws of the Vampires. So, if I say these attacks will cease, then they will." My voice came across strong and loud, and not a single word trembled.

The Commissioner paused in his tracks and turned to face me. He stared at me for the longest moment and then uttered two words loud enough for the entire room to hear. "Prove it."

Then he left.

Taking with him my fleeting flare of pride and purpose.

I glanced at his hand, and the terror that file contained.

I would.

I would prove what I had to.

And be damned with the rest.

CHAPTER SEVEN

HIDDEN KISSES, HIDDEN AGENDAS

"What's he doing here?" Chuck snapped, staring at Judas as he climbed out of his sports car parked across the road from my parents' house.

I shut the door of the family limo in the driveway and waved at the handsome Wolf as he glanced my way and winked, melting the legs right out from under me. "I messaged him to meet me here. I need a lift back to the Academy after we meet with Mom and the other Vamps. You said you had an errand to run."

Chuck glanced my way with an arched brow and wore an exasperated expression. "I didn't say I wasn't going to give you a lift back."

Ava climbed out of the limo on the other side and stared at Judas. "What's he doing here?"

I rolled my eyes. "You two go inside and tell Mom I'll be there in a sec."

"She's not going to be happy with all the guests already here." He eyed the expensive cars lining the street, Mercedes, Lamborghinis, and even a shiny purple Bugatti.

Yep, Mom would get frustrated and her cheeks would

glow red because she was the ultimate party planner and everything had to go perfectly. I'd asked her to quickly call the most influential Vamps over for an urgent meeting. The conference with the humans hadn't gone exactly as planned, but it opened my eyes to how much I had to step up without Dad around. I intended to keep my word and have that police commissioner eat his words for ever doubting me.

"Let's leave the love birds." Ava looped an arm around Chuck's and walked toward my parents' grand mansion. The place had dark pointy towers that always reminded me of a birthday cake. Mom insisted it was a palace, while Dad called it his crown.

"Hey, babe." Judas took my hand when he reached me and drew me against him, his arm wrapped around my back. "You did amazing at the conference. So proud of how you stood up to the commissioner."

I drowned in his chocolate eyes, his words covering me in goosebumps. "I was nervous as hell."

"Couldn't tell."

I leaned closer, and my cheek pressed to his chest. I listened to the thundering of his pulse. He kissed the top of my head. For those few moments, I wanted to freeze time and pretend all the other crap in my world didn't exist. That I just attended the Academy and my biggest problem was getting more time with my Wolves.

Someone cleared their throat nearby, and I pulled myself out of Judas' arms to see a familiar face. Mariana, the wife of Mihai the Immortal, a name which made me giggle every time he introduced himself. *Hello*, all Vamps were immortal.

Mariana snarled when she glared at Judas, having sensed he was a Wolf. Vampires and Werewolves didn't mix... except, I planned to change that perception, to help rewire the misconceptions. Which I knew was an uphill battle, especially with the older generation like Mariana who hissed at Judas, her fangs on display, before turning and marching toward the house with her purse tucked tightly under her arm.

"Gah, just ignore her," I murmured.

Judas shrugged, clearly unaffected and I appreciated that. "Come, let's get you inside before your mom sends an army out after you."

He took my hand and we waltzed up the driveway. I guided him around the side of the house to the kitchen entrance where I'd sneak in without drawing attention.

At the door, Judas grabbed my hips and turned me to face him. I gasped as he walked me backward until I hit the wall, and his lips were on mine in seconds. Deep and passionate, he pressed his tongue against the seam of my lips and I took him into my mouth. Shaking all over from his forcefulness, I adored him manhandling me.

He tasted like peppermint. I leaned into him, combing my fingers through his dark hair, wanting us closer. Something about kissing secretly while the Vamps remained inside burned me up with excitement. Mom would be mortified, but I'd rather remain here, glued to Judas, than inside. Unfortunately, my logical mind reminded me of my responsibility, my duty, of Dad's plight. And that drenched me in icy water, so I broke free from Judas' arms.

"I should head inside." I still held onto his arms, not ready to go.

"I know. When you're ready, I'll be waiting in the car." He offered me his smile again, standing in front of me in his black shirt and cuffs, black jeans, and hell, he was so gorgeous. All angles and strong features, I drew him closer for a quick kiss, and his warmth spread through me.

"You don't want to come inside?" I breathed.

"See you soon, babe. Good luck." He broke free from my hold and walked away. My gaze fell on how perfectly his jeans hugged his ass. I still tasted him, and I'd love to have him by my side during this meeting. But he was right. That would only lead to problems.

So, I squared my shoulders and headed inside, needing to get this over with.

Helene, the family helper was rushing out of the room with a silver platter filled with tiny treats and into my Dad's meeting room. Ava was standing with the fridge door open, staring inside. She glanced over her shoulder at me and sighed.

"No chocolate. What house doesn't have chocolate in the house?"

"A Vampire's house."

She shut the door. "Considering you have gross jellied blood shots in the fridge for guests, you should have the good stuff too."

"Dad has a stash for when shifters come over." I headed to the pantry and pulled it open then walked inside the small room with Ava on my heels.

"Holy crap, this is bigger than my dorm. Why do you have all these foods if you only drink blood?"

"We sometimes mix blood with foods, plus, Mom entertains a lot!"

I reached over to a shelf stacked high with full sized chocolate bars and grabbed the top one before handing it over. "Here you go. We're not all monsters."

She creased her nose. "Really? Dark chocolate. You are

a monster." With a grin, she nudged past me and went through the stack, pulling out three packets.

"These are for Ron." She smirked and headed out.

"Ron? You didn't keep one of those demonic bunnies as your pet?" I shut the door as Helene returned to the kitchen, glaring at me for going into her pantry.

"For later'on," Ava corrected me, already tearing open the rocky road chocolate.

"That's a terrible joke." I rolled my eyes when Helene rushed to my side, reprimanding me with her glare.

"Mistress, you must hurry. They are waiting for you. Your mother will scream at all of us."

"Yeah, hurry up, Mistress." Ava giggled to herself before stuffing the sweet stuff into her mouth.

I swallowed the lump in my throat and hurried toward the board room. The white walls were covered in family portraits, and I cringed at seeing myself at barely thirty years old, hair in pigtails, and braces. Hell, I told Dad to take that photo down.

Everyone stared my way. Twenty Vamps sat around the long mahogany table, sipping blood from crystal glasses and nibbling on tiny blood-infused cheese on crackers.

"About time." Mom marched over to me, her arms swinging by her sides, and her usually perfect hair sat slightly messy, a couple of strands sticking out of the bun at the back of her head.

She seized my wrist, her fingernails digging into my flesh and walked me to the other end of the room.

"You sure took your time outside," she whispered, cutting me a sharp look.

She must have seen me out there with Judas. She looked at me for a moment, her eyes almost glistening like she was beside herself, barely keeping it together.

"I've got this Mom."

And as she stared at me, her flushed expression melted away, replaced with a perfect smile, her tense posture easing. She spun on her heels to face the room, greeting them with her spectacular fake grin.

"You all know my incredibly talented daughter, who is not only in line to take over the Livingstone business, but was recently appointed as Understudy. So, her word is as good as the Ancient's."

Everyone gave me a small clap, but I couldn't get over the words about me taking over Dad's business. I mean, I knew, but to hear it said like that made it way too real.

Mom slid into a spare seat at the table, crossed her legs, and placed her clasped hands in the lap of her white leather straight skirt.

I remained standing; this was a talk that required authority. I spent the first few moments sweeping my gaze across the room, meeting everyone's eyes, acknowledging I recognized each of them. When I landed on Ava, she was covering her mouth, sniggering to herself with her eyes glued to the portrait of me in pigtails. Hell, I was tossing that thing out today.

"Thank you all for attending on such short notice. I won't take much of your time, but I just came back from a conference with the human spokesman. The mortals are afraid and upset about the sudden Vampire attacks on their kind."

Mariana's mouth opened, with what I could only image was a protest about a lack of blood, but I jumped in before she could.

"Yes, we are having some blood shortage issues, but we are working on that. I told them the illness was over, and they have nothing to fear."

"How can you make such a claim? Isn't your father still sick?" Mariana spat the words.

All I saw in my mind's eye was Dad, chained up, the animal in his eyes, in his voice. That wasn't my dad. I'd find a way to help him.

"And I heard the infection started from the Wolves. Dirty animals who smell and poo everywhere." She glared at me, her eyes narrowing, and the silence between us spoke loudly.

"Vampires, Wolves, we are all Supernatural and affected the same way. We need to work as a collective. So I'm asking you if you know who's behind these attacks on the mortals? Whoever it is, these attacks need to stop. And I'm depending on you, and as the Understudy, I'm depending on you to make sure these don't happen again."

No one said a word, just stared at me with big eyes. All these men and women dressed in their best, most expensive clothes would do anything to avoid resorting to their pure animalistic sides.

"It's up to us, the powerful families amid the masses to make a difference." *Always placate the rich families,* Dad would say. *It is the best way to get them to do anything you wanted.*

I continued and explained the photos they showed me at the conference, needing them to understand the dire situation and how quickly this could spiral out of control.

After answering a number of questions which all revolved around blood supply, I helped Mom see everyone out of the house.

Once she shut the door, I flopped onto the couch in the main entertaining room. "Let's never do that again."

"Girl, you were amazing. All serious and almost like a robot." Ava stuffed more chocolate into her mouth.

"A robot? And you're gonna make yourself sick."

Mom sat next to me, taking my hand in hers. "Your dad would be so proud. I don't know where this new, confident Morwenna has come from, but I like it." She drew me into her arms, and I held her, feeling her body give a slight tremble.

"Everything's going to be alright, you'll see," I offered.

She pulled back and faced me. "I keep thinking back, trying to remember what signs I missed of him getting sick so I can pinpoint what he'd done beforehand. But all I keep remembering is this strange new mark he had on his shoulder blade. It had a blue glow and was circular. I don't know what it was."

"Everyone is working on this, the Wolves and Witches. We'll find a solution soon. Though not sure I trust Mariana. She had attitude today."

Mom stood and brushed down her skirt with shaky hands. "Come, I'll bring us all a cup of my relaxing tea. We could all do with some. Chuck, go call Morwenna's Wolf friend from the car to join us."

I cringed, and then shot a glance to Ava...*what the fuck? A Wolf...invited into my home by my Mom?*

The warrior followed her command, while Ava crashed down onto the opposite couch, admiring the wallpaper, the chandelier. "Pretty ritzy in here. You should see my dad's palace, it'd blow you away."

I adored having Ava with me, as she took the edge off everything. "It's not a competition," I murmured.

"Exactly, it's not. Anyway, if we stay tonight, we're gonna be pretty late to classes tomorrow. And anyway, have you seen the new principal?" She picked up a magazine from the coffee table and flicked through it.

"No, although he seems to be making his presence known."

She shrugged and dumped the magazine back. "Someone was saying he's a hard ass. Not sure if that means he has a firm butt or is a bit of a dictator."

"Hopefully not the latter." I wasn't sure I was ready to deal with another principal considering the last one tried to kill me.

CHAPTER EIGHT

IT'S ALLERGY SEASON

"Livingstone! Stop right there!" The deafening boom tore through the hallway.

I glanced at my classroom at the other end of the hallway and stilled, salvation just out of reach.

Footsteps thundered behind me. I thought I could slip around the corner and escape. I thought wrong.

"Where have you been?"

I turned, lifted my gaze and met the burning stare of Principal Balefire. "I had to attend a meeting, Sir."

"What kind of meeting?" he snapped and stared down at me.

I hated being looked down on. I'd had it all my life, the smiles, the condescending tones. The pats on the arms. *There's a good dear.* "An Understudy mee—"

"You know what?" He shook his head. "I don't care. Your problems are not my problems Livingstone, and neither are they this school's."

"I never said—"

He held up a hand, cutting me off and leaned down to glare harder. "You might've had sway here before, but you'll have none anymore. Keep your Vampire problems out of my face. And no more missing classes. The next time I see you in this hallway after the bell has rung, you'll be serving detention. Do you understand me?"

I just stared at him. *You've got to be kidding, right?* Anger boiled to the surface. "My father—"

Something bareled around the corner of the hallway at break-neck speed and slammed into Principal Balefire. He stumbled forward with an *oof,* and wrenched his gaze to Nesrin as she jerked her head up in surprise.

"Sorry," she muttered and kept on walking.

"Wait a minute," Balefire snarled and whipped his gaze toward her.

Green eyes flashed with defiance as she whipped long, ebony hair from her shoulders. "Yes?"

"Why are *you* out of class?"

She never answered, only met his searing gaze with her own. Her lips curled, the birth of a snarl just waiting to break free.

"Are you..." he started and then stilled. His nose scrunched, Hellfire blazed just a little brighter in his eyes. "I...ah." His eyes closed, there was a tremor for a second before he straightened, jerked his head backwards and let out the loudest sneeze. *"Wherechoo!"* A damn fireball the size of my head shot from his lips, hurled across the hallway to smash into the wall.

The bitter scent of burning wood and plasterboard filled the hall. I covered my nose, and Nesrin followed. "What the hell," she muttered.

"Wherechoo...wherechoo...argh!" He stumbled backwards, fireballs slamming into doors and flying through the air as he glared from me to Nesrin. "I'm allergic to damn cats!"

"Nice one," I murmured, earning a snarl from Nesrin as she took a step toward the Principal. "And I don't like *Hounds* either."

"Go." Balefire shooed us away with the wave of his hand. "Don't...*wherechoo!* Don't let me see you out...*wherechoo!*"

He stumbled away from us, actually holding his nose and sniffing.

"You've got to be shitting me," she snarled.

I turned away, hurrying for the classroom.

"Wait." She reached out, grabbed my arm, stopping me cold.

No goddamn way. Not again. I was in no mood for her shit. "Look..."

"I'm sorry," she started.

The words dried up in my mouth. "You're what now?"

"Taking your ring wasn't my idea," she started, lowered her gaze to her hand on my arm and then removed it. "Just wanted you to know."

I was silent for a second. What was she up to? This wasn't the bitchy Nesrin I knew. "I know, but thank you."

"I don't want there to be any bad blood between us, not after the dance you know?"

She almost looked embarrassed. "Thank you," I murmured. "I appreciate it. Do you know where Brylee is now?"

"No idea. She ran away after the dance and haven't seen her since." Then there was a nod, and an awkward glance toward the door of the classroom before she shuffled off. I followed, earning a glare from Mrs. Kent. "Nice of you to join us."

I glanced at Ava who glared to Nesrin as I slid into the seat beside her.

"What was that about?" she murmured.

"I'll tell you later," I answered, unable to believe the conversation myself.

"Right, now that we have everyone here, I have an announcement."

The classroom door opened once more and a waif slipped in, head down, long brown hair hiding her face from us. Mrs. Kent glanced her way, waved her forward. "We have a new student, Huntleigh Blackthorne, please do your best to welcome her. And with that we'll be paring up into twos for this next lesson."

The class moaned, and a few students shook their heads. I glanced at Ava, and she shifted toward me.

"Ava, you'll be pairing up with Kysen on this one."

Ava closed her eyes, inhaled hard and then turned to the front of the class. "Why?"

Mrs. Kent never answered, only caught my gaze and nodded. "Morwenna, you'll be with Huntleigh. I expect you'll be able to show her a little of the school. I want each pair to go outside and let their instinct take them some-where they've never been before."

"Out of this class?" someone muttered.

They earned a savage glare. "I expect you to be on your best behaviour, explore the grounds, but go no further. I want each of you to come back and give a ten minute talk on where your instinct led you and why. We need to learn to not just listen to that primal voice inside us, but to question, to use it to our advantage, and have the common sense to turn away when it's not to our advantage."

"This is bullshit," Ava grunted and glanced to Kysen who just glared at her from across the class.

No one wanted to be partnered with the Banshee. In fact, no one wanted to be anywhere near her, even the school didn't want her here. But her parents had forced them, and now we all walked on eggshells—no one wanted to hear a Banshee's scream. Poor Ava.

I glanced to the new girl with straight brown hair and a very familiar name, then caught her shyly lift her gaze. There was a second where we connected, before her breath caught and her eyes widened.

Then I forced a smile and slid from my seat.

"Okay, let your instinct lead the way, and then come back and prepare for a ten minute speech on what led you, where it led you, what was the primary reason, and what was the outcome."

No one was happy, least of all Ava. She just strode toward the door, not bothering to wait for Kysen. The white haired Banshee followed, glaring at everyone around her and snarled, "Get the hell outta my way."

Ava was going to have so much fun.

"Hi." I neared the new student. "I'm Morwenna, but most people just call me Mor."

"Huntleigh," she muttered. "I'm sorry, but I have no idea what I'm doing here."

"It's all good." I motioned to the spare desk behind mine. "Want to drop your bag and we can head out?"

There was a shake of her head. Her hand went to the strap over her shoulder and gripped tight.

"Okay," I murmured. Weird. "Let's do this."

She followed me out of the door and into the hallway where plumes of white smoke filled the hall. The wall still smouldered from the Principal's allergies. So, the Hellhound couldn't be near any cats...*interesting*.

"I'm guessing you know my cousin, Judas," she blurted.

"Huh?" I wrenched my gaze from the smoking plaster to her.

"My cousin, Judas. I'm guessing you know him," she rephrased.

"I do." I tried to keep my feelings about him hidden. "He's a...friend."

We followed the chatter and the booming sound of a herd of jostling, chattering supernaturals toward the guard at the front door of the building. He glared at us, dark eyes burning with red flames as we passed.

Judas hadn't told me his cousin was coming to the Academy, or maybe he didn't know.

"So, what made you decide to come to Bestias?" I glanced from one of the many guards now positioned around the grounds to Ava as she disappeared through the doorway and Kysen followed.

"Just felt like it was time. I saw you, you know that, right? The other night, with Judas at his parents' house."

I shoved through the door and stepped out into the sunlight. And with her words, that night rushed back. But it wasn't the woods, the house, or a hundred other things from that night that consumed me. It was the look on my father's face as he thrashed against the binds and the spell. It was that savageness, that desperation and underneath it—there was fear.

"You didn't see me," she kept on talking as we walked. "But I saw you. I saw the way you walked in with him, and then the way you walked out. You shouldn't give yourself over to him so easily. You shouldn't..."

I stopped in the middle of the path, and then turned to face this strange girl. "Look, I get you're trying to look out for me. But I don't even know you. Judas has been nothing but supportive and to me that's what a friend is."

"He's not told you, has he?" Her deep brown eyes grew darker in the sunlight, until they were almost black.

"Told me what?" She just held my gaze. I didn't know if I liked her, didn't know if I wanted to start down the path of not liking her. "Either tell me, or leave it alone."

She swallowed hard, gripped her pack and...waited.

"That's what I thought," I murmured and then strode away.

At this point I'd rather have the screaming, damn Banshee for a partner. I tried to search for Ava and the others but they were long gone. It looked like I was left with the weird girl. I sighed, turned and faced her. "Look, you don't need to worry. I'm a big girl, I can look after myself."

She just gave a shrug and mumbled, "Suit yourself."

"Right, we're supposed to do this. Did you want to take a walk around the grounds?"

"Or I can meet you somewhere," she murmured and looked toward the Lodge.

"Sure," I muttered. "Meet you at the pond behind the main building if you want?"

She was already moving, striding away from me. I just shook my head and watched her leave. "Whatever."

It was supposed to be a partnered task, but the new girl rubbed me the wrong way, no matter who her cousin was. To be honest, I'd rather be alone. Movement behind me drew my gaze. I glanced over my shoulder to the guard standing inside the doorway, until she veered off the path, then I headed for the library. Instinct was supposed to lead me, but I had no idea where. I glanced left, catching sight of Huntleigh as she slipped around the corner of the hall.

And my instinct flared.

My steps slowed, gaze narrowed. I no longer cared about the library, or anything else for that matter. The hairs on the nape of my neck rose as I stepped off the path, following her around the end of the hall.

The side door was open, darkness waiting inside. I tried to move, but the past waited, reaching me like a tsunami.

All I could see was blood and darkness. All I could hear were the screams as the Demons attacked. It all happened, right in there. I wanted to turn away, wanted to let that screaming voice inside me to take over. I wanted to run, but for some reason I couldn't. Instead I stepped forward, catching movement inside.

I stopped at the wall, easing forward to peek inside. She was there...the strange new girl, crouched on the floor. I stepped forward, slipping in. I didn't care if she saw me now. I only wanted to see what she was doing.

Her head was down. She was focussed on scraping something from the floor. The corner of a white envelope snagged my attention. I glanced around the room, remembering exactly where everyone had been.

But I knew she was standing where I had when the Demons attacked.

Right where the Dragon Tears turned to dust and floated to the floor.

It'd been what...weeks since the attack. The floor must've been cleaned, three...*four* times since then? Still, she found something, using the edge of a blade to drive between the cracks of the floor and scoop something free.

"What are you doing?"

She jerked her head up at the sound. There was a flare of surprise, before a shake of her head. Whatever was on the end of her knife was tipped into the worn envelope. She folded the top over before rising to stand.

"Nothing." She shoved the envelope into her backpack, and folded down the blade of the knife before stowing it away.

"It doesn't look like nothing. Looks like you're scraping something from the floor. What is it?"

"You know what it is." She met my gaze and strode forward, one hand on the back of her pack.

"Hey." I reached out and grabbed her arm as she passed.

I had her all wrong. She wasn't shy. She wasn't quiet. She was a damn viper in waiting.

She looked down at my grip on her arm and spoke, "I'm not your enemy here, Morwenna."

"Then stop acting like it." I let her go. "Because the damn wait list is getting too long."

Footsteps sounded outside. Chatter spilled into the dance hall as the other students strode past.

"Better get back to class." Huntleigh took a step toward the doorway.

I let her go, no matter how desperate I was. She slipped from the hall before I knew, then I had no choice but to follow her back to class.

We strode in with the others, and by then the first student was giving a blow by blow enactment of how he allowed his instinct to hunt town a small mouse scurrying through the trees.

"Gross," Ava muttered and crossed her arms.

Others followed, standing up in front of the class. Luckily only one of the pair had to give the talk. When Mrs. Kent glanced our way, I motioned for Huntleigh to take her shot.

If she wanted to lie to my face, then she'd get no help from me.

She was a skilled liar, I'll give her that. Standing in front of the class, putting on the shy, mumbling face once more that drew pity from the teacher as she smiled and motioned for her to sit.

When the bell rang, I was the first one out of the room.

"What the Hell was that?" Ava snarled in my ear.

"A lying, conniving bitch, that's what," I answered and pushed through the front doors of the building.

Ava hung back, giving me some space. I needed it. I was *fuming*. I strode around the grounds, eyed the hall once more, and then headed for my dorm. Huntleigh Blackthorne had got under my skin. I didn't know why, but she did...and I wanted her out.

CHAPTER NINE

FAMILY AFFAIRS

"Hey, Mor. Wait up," Nero called from behind me.

I glanced over my shoulder as he raced across the grounds from the cafeteria. Arms swung by his side, and for some absurd reason, I tried really hard to picture him running without a shirt. All muscles, his tanned skin rippling with perspiration, his abs hard.

"Been calling you for ages, where are you going in such a rush, babe?"

"Babe?"

He leaned in closer, his mouth grazing mine, his hands cupping the sides of my face. A furnace erupted within me, and I plastered my palms against his rock hard chest.

"Get a room," someone growled as they rushed past, and I broke Nero's gaze to find the Banshee, Kysen. The pale-haired waif curled her top lip in a sneer.

"Where are you headed?"

"To my room," The furnace of rage simmered just under the surface. "To get away from Huntleigh Blackthorne."

He flinched with the name and straightened. "Judas said that she might be attending here. Did she...*did she hurt you?*" His gaze went to the drop of blood on my white school shirt and tartan tie.

I rubbed the stain over my heart. "No, that was me." I held up my hand, the crimson moon still welled in the center of my palm. "But she was the damn cause."

He just nodded and glanced away. "She has a knack for being a pain in the ass. Sorry you got on the wrong side of her. She's...troubled, so we all try to make allowances."

"Troubled, how?" I searched my memory.

"That's a story for another time." He shook his head and answered. "I'll join you, if you're heading to your dorm."

"You sure about that?" I glared at the towering guard as he strode along the footpath, checking the Academy grounds. We couldn't move in this place anymore without being watched. Suspicion haunted me.

Even the sun didn't seem as warm as it'd been before.

"I've been wanting to talk to you without the others," he started and glanced my way. "I wanted to see how you were, you know, after the attack."

He didn't know I'd seen the woman in black.

Not many people did.

"I'm not going to lie." I glanced his way, watching for his reaction. "I've had some lingering problems."

Concern flared across his face as he reached for my hand. "You can always talk to me, you know? You can tell me anything, about your dad, or your powers. I just don't want you to feel like you're alone in any of this."

He reached for the door to my dorm and yanked. I stilled halfway inside. Desire mingled with a tremble of need, and I rose on my toes to kiss him against his cheek.

I inhaled the scent of his Wolf, lifting my hand to slide my fingers along his cheek. His breath hot against my skin.

He lowered his head, but it had nothing to do with being submissive, and everything to do with desire.

"You make me crazy." The growl was nothing more than a murmur as he brushed his lips against my neck, and then pulled away, eyes burning neon blue.

Heat raced through my veins, and my quiet heart gave a shudder.

I gave him a hint of a smile, before stepping through the open door and heading inside. Our footsteps echoed as we climbed the stairs. I caught movement in the shadows, before Nero growled, "Mom?"

Silver hair glinted in the dim light as she stepped out, eyes frozen on us.

"What are you doing here?" Nero surged forward. "Is something wrong?"

"We need to talk." She cut a glance at me. "You too."

Pendants clicked and clattered around her neck as she moved. Her long, black flowing skirt skimmed the floor, and the purple crocheted top looked too cool for someone with warm blood in their veins.

I stilled at the last stair and motioned to my room. "Do you want to come inside?"

She followed, reaching out for Nero's hand as she passed.

"Is Dad okay?" Concern consumed his face.

"Yes...*yes*, it's nothing like that." She shook her head and turned, standing in the middle of my room. "It's just, I want you to come with me."

"Come with you? Why?" Nero stilled.

"I think...I think you need to stay away from the Black-thorne Wolves right now. Both of you. I can figure out something to tell your Principal, something that will explain both of your absences. I can make up something, some family member died. I'm sure she'll understand."

"He," Nero answered. "The Principal is a he now?"

She just nodded, frantic gaze flitting around my room. There was something she wasn't telling us.

"Talk to us." I searched her gaze. "Tell us what's wrong."

"I had a dream last night. A terrible, dark dream." She shook her head, wringing her hands. "I can't have anything happening to you. I just can't...."

"What are you talking about, Mom?"

She shook her head. "I had a dream that something terrible happened to you...to the both of you, and you know the dreams I'm talking about Nero. *A Witch's dream.*"

"A prophecy?" I whispered.

His mom looked over to us. "I'm sorry about your father, Morwenna." A shadow crossed her face. "But there's no stopping this curse, and the blood of my blood was never involved."

"Involved in what?" I asked.

She shook her head and turned to face the balcony, staring out into the field below. I moved toward her. I stepped closer, reaching out to take her hand. "*What was the dream?*"

Power danced across her skin, like a hundred cuts. I hissed and pulled away. She'd never felt this strong before. "Why the sudden increase in power? What are you hiding?"

Her sleeve rode up as she nervously brushed strands of her hair from her face. Thick black bands were drawn across her skin in symbols that looked familiar. "Protection." I lifted my gaze to her eyes. "That's what they mean, right?"

She glanced to Nero, and then closed her eyes with a shake of her head. "I saw a house in the Moors, a cottage, one that's haunted by a Witch. A Witch who's blood was spilled there. A Witch who cursed the Livingstone name, and the Blackthorne's. She's angry, Nero." Fear darkened her eyes. "She's so angry. She's marked those she's going to take, and there's nothing you can do to stop her."

Marked?

That was the second time I'd heard those words. "What mark?"

"All I know is what the dream showed me. I saw a couple in love...a young Witch, just starting to find her powers. But then the man she loved betrayed her...and then he cursed her. I woke up screaming names...*Hawke...Blackthorne...Livingstone...*"

I flinched with her words. That couldn't be. Not us, not my family. "It's just a dream," I muttered.

"These are not just any dreams Morwenna," she snarled. "These are *warnings*. You'd best listen."

"Moors, you said." I held her gaze.

"Sommersbey's Moors," she answered and gripped my arms. "I'm telling you this so you can get as far away from that place *and* your own blood as possible."

"Please, Nero. I'm begging."

He looked at me, as though trying to decide. "I'm going," I turned and met his gaze. "I *have too*. But you don't. You can go with your Mom."

I took a step away from him, trying my best to make him see. This wasn't a battle, this was about love.

"I'm sorry, Mom." He croaked holding my gaze. "But I have to. I won't let someone I care about fight this on their own."

"You're just like your father. Stubborn to a fault. It will

get you killed, Nero...it'll leave you in a misty place with the dead."

He swallowed hard. "Then I'll take that chance."

She didn't answer, only nodded her head and walked slowly out of the room...alone.

"Sorry you had to see that." He turned away from me.

The terrifying image of Judas' father filled me. Clawed out eyes, shattered hands. My stomach clenched in warning. "I'm going to the Moors. I'm going to figure this out and put a stop to it once and for all."

One nod was all he gave. "What do you need me to do?"

I met those hard eyes and answered. "Chuck will know what to do." I dug into my pocket, yanked out my phone, and sent the big brute a message.

Mor: Coming to your place. We have a plan. Be ready for a trip.

Beep.

Chuck: You'd better have a damn good reason.

I stared at the message. I did have a damn good reason.

My father's life.

And then I messaged the others, telling them to meet me at Chuck's. "There." I slipped the cell into my pocket once more. "It's done."

"You ready?" He reached out his hand.

I took his comfort and strength, slipping my fingers between his as he yanked open my bedroom door. We made our way down to the foyer, and then out of the dorm, heading for the small cottage on the edge of the Academy grounds, and for once there wasn't a surly looking Hellhound guard in sight.

One glance around us, and Nero opened the front door to Chuck's little cottage and stepped inside. I could already hear their chatter waiting for me, Ava's voice the loudest of all as she snapped, *"Look, we just wait and hear what she has to say, okay?"*

They all turned toward us, Judas's gaze narrowing on Nero, and then to me.

The Alpha just waited.

"Nero's Mom paid me a visit." Eyebrows raised around the room. I had everyone's attention. "She had a dream of a Witch betrayed by her lover. It seems her blood was spilled at a cottage out in the Moors. And three names were cursed: Hawke's, Blackthorne's, and Livingstone's. Sound familiar?"

There wasn't a word, until Chuck muttered, "And you believe her?"

"I believe we have a name of a place and the Witch who betrayed her."

"Where?" Chuck growled.

"Sommersbey Moors," Nero answered.

There was a flinch from Chuck. Judas seemed to pale. Bond was the only one who spoke. "I think I know where that is."

"You mean, you know the place?" A chilling breath came at the nape of my neck.

"I have a map." Chuck turned and strode out of the room and returned a second later carrying a large treasure chest of rolled maps, the old fashioned kind I'd only ever seen in movies. He dumped them on the sofa. Why did he own that?

"It's in here somewhere," he mumbled to himself.

"Never knew you collected maps," Ava cooed, leaning back in her chair, balancing on the two back legs, gawking at Chuck's ass he bent at the waist, searching through the maps.

I kicked her under the table, and she started falling backward, her eyes widening, her arms flapping.

Bond snatched her elbow and tugged her back, the chair thumping down. She gasped for air and glared at me.

"That's evil. I could have died."

Bond burst out laughing, while Nero and Judas sat there in silence, both of them with solemn expressions.

"Okay." Chuck stood up from the box, clutching a huge rolled up map. "I found Sommersbey's. I've been there once." Chuck pulled up a chair and rolled out the map across the table. Everyone reached out, grabbing an end to keep it flat, and we all stared down at enormous green landscape. Mountains, trees, houses on the outskirts of the woods. And within the forest, half a dozen trails, some crossing each other.

"So, what are we looking for?" Chuck asked.

"A cottage," I suggested and everyone but Nero looked up at me with a *are you kidding me* look.

"There are no cottages on this drawing." Ava pointed to the map.

I shrugged. "Well, that Forsaken Witch lived there, so maybe we'll find something there to help us. It's the only lead we've got so far. Better than doing nothing."

"Dad once told me about a cottage in the woods that belonged to a Witch," Bond added, and every eye in the room shot to him as he raked a hand through his golden hair.

Silence swept through the room, until a sudden snarl came from the hall.

We all jumped as the snarl grew louder. Judas had his hand on my thigh, firm and ready to protect me. A girl could get used to this.

The energy in the room suddenly went from playful to tense as hell.

Claws scratching wood escalated, and in a heartbeat,

something the size of a Dachshund shot out from the hallway and into the room with us, rolling around wildly.

Ava screamed and jumped onto her seat, while everyone else leaped to their feet.

We all stared at the furball that suddenly halted and tottered around with its black face and white markings. A pair of blue striped boxers dangled from his mouth.

"Jabba!" Chuck yelled and climbed to his feet. "I told you to stay out of my room."

My birthday present from Dad snarled, black lips curled back over sharp little fangs that pierced Chuck's underwear. The warrior lunged but the badger was too fast, scrambling out of reach and dropped the Vampire's striped boxers. Chuck and the badger both vanished around the corner, heavy footfalls swallowed by a roar of desperation in the other room.

Something crashed to the floor with a *boom!*

Ava leaped to her feet and darted after him.

The Wolves were howling in laughter, and it was contagious. My belly jiggled, as a giggle slipped from my lips.

"That's it, I've had it with that chipmunk," Chuck growled from the doorway, his hair falling over his eyes. The warrior a little out of breath. "He's your problem from now on. You're taking him."

"Maybe he just needs one of those outdoor cages where he can play. He probably gets bored," Ava suggested as she stepped alongside Chuck. "Anyway, he's closed in the bathroom for now."

With Ava back at the table, Chuck brought us all cans of soda and took his seat again, downing his can of beer in a few mouthfuls.

"Okay, back to the cottage," Chuck stated, and we all turned our attention to Bond.

He shrugged. "Dad mentioned a cottage somewhere in the woods and how it was super creepy and apparently haunted."

"And, where is it located?" I jabbed a finger at the map, hitting it square in the middle of the woods.

He shrugged. "I'll have to call home and find out. You sure this is the right thing? I've heard so many bad things about these woods."

"Think hard about this, Morwenna." Chuck brushed the hair from his eyes.

"Stories originate from some place, right?" I muttered and stared at the map. "So that's what we do, we find out if this story is what's making my dad sick. So, who's in?"

"Me...*me*...Hell yeah," they echoed in unison.

"Bond, you find the location from your parents, and Chuck we're gonna need the limo. Now, exactly how far are these woods from here?"

"Limo's not going to go where we're going." Bond chuckled. "You're gonna need four wheel drives."

That bad? I glanced at the map and then lifted my gaze to a grinning Bond. "Oh yeah." He nodded. "We're about to get a little muddy."

CHAPTER TEN

MUD, BLOOD, AND BROKEN SORROWS

MORNING ROSE WITH A CRIMSON SKY SPLASHED ACROSS the horizon. I prayed it wasn't an omen. I turned away from the terrifying sunrise and climbed into the towering beast of a car. I'd never been in a vehicle like this. Dad would be horrified. But I just swallowed and climbed in, yanking the door shut behind me with a *bang*.

"You good?" Bond growled and leaned across the passenger's seat to grab the seatbelt. "You're gonna need this."

An engine started behind us with a snarl. I glanced in the side mirror to Chuck and Ava in the gleaming black Hummer behind us. The Vampire warrior insisted on taking his own car. We only needed one of us to get into trouble, and we'd have to leave someone behind, was his reasoning.

I think he secretly wanted time with Ava. And I wanted to be here, right up front, desperate to find the origin of this story.

"Yeah, I'm good."

Green eyes sparkled with excitement as he started the truck and the engine growled, throbbing with need.

"You're safe with me." He shoved the truck into gear, glanced into the rear view mirror and pulled out.

"I know." I swallowed a shudder and watched the familiar sight of the Academy gates come closer.

Bond handled the four wheel drive like he'd been born behind the wheel, taking a right out of the Academy gates.

Nero and Judas relaxed in the backseat. I'd had to fight them for shot-gun, wanting to see everything.

"You think Balefire is going to chuck a shit-fit?" Nero muttered and glanced toward me.

I just nodded. "There's no doubt. I just hope to God he doesn't call your damn parents."

"Not much sense in calling mine," Bond muttered and hit the turn signal, pulling us onto the highway in the opposite direction of the city. "Dad's probably sleeping a hard night off with another damn mortal. I doubt he'd get the reception he was after."

I winced with his words.

"Mom will be gone now," Nero added. "So, there's no answer there."

"None for me either." Judas just sat back in the seat. "So, I'd say we're in the clear."

Trees whipped by. I glanced into the side mirror every now and then and relaxed as Bond headed further south.

"I'm sorry about your dad." I glanced toward him.

He met my gaze and forced a smile. "Don't worry about it, I'm not. My family is the Blackthorne pack anyway." He glanced into the rear view mirror and raised his fist.

"Amen, brother," Judas growled behind me, leaning through the gap in the seat to bump his fist.

Still, I couldn't imagine that. I'd been sheltered my

entire life, unable to look past the mirage of perfection. How petty and selfish I'd been.

"We'll figure this out," Nero said, drawing my gaze.

I just nodded and eased back in the seat. Bond leaned forward, hit the button on the stereo and the hard rock beat of Dorothy filled the interior.

Hours passed rocking out to one beat after another as the trees around us grew smaller, and finally gave way to rolling hills and lush green grass.

"Gonna have to stop, up ahead." Bond glanced at the fuel gauge.

Storm clouds climbed over the horizon toward us looking bruised and angry. I grabbed my phone and sent Ava a text.

Mor: Gonna stop for fuel soon. How is it?

Beep.

Ava: It's very...*very growly.*

I winced at the response, not wanting to read too much into it and lowered my phone.

Beep.

Ava: Chuck said he has his eye on those Wolves, but don't worry. I'll keep the big brute occupied for you.

I chuckled and shook my head.

"What's so funny?" Judas called from the rear seat.

"Ava and Chuck, the most unlikely pair to get together." I tucked my phone away.

"What's the deal with those two, anyway?" Bond glanced my way

I met his gaze. "I have no idea, and I'm not quite certain I want to know."

He just laughed, hit the turn signal and a small, rundown gas station came into view. Dust kicked up behind us as he pulled up next to the bowser. I shoved open the door and climbed out.

The sweet scent of the storm cut through the dust. Frigid wind whipped the remnant away as the Chuck pulled the Hummer in behind us. Ava opened the door and climbed out, casually making her way toward me.

"You good?" She brushed hair from my shoulders.

"Yep." I met her gaze. "How about a chocolate bar, my treat?"

"Then I'll have two." She giggled and turned toward the small, decrepit store.

Thick paint flaked off the metal handle of the place as I opened the door and strode through.

No Vamps.
No Immortales.
By Management

Said from the sign above the counter. I winced at the spelling.

"Well, shit," muttered Ava. "Lucky we're not Immortales, hey?" She just shook her head and ignored the sign.

There was a grunt from behind the counter and an old man stood. He turned critical eyes on Ava first, and then me.

"You a Vamp?" he snarled at my best friend.

"Nope," she muttered, and grabbed two chocolate bars from the dusty box on the shelf.

The door opened with a *scrape,* and I turned as Chuck squeezed through the doorway and strode through the store.

"But he is," she added with a smirk. "You gonna take our money, old timer? We don't want any trouble."

He just stared at the warrior as he reached into his

pocket and peeled off a ten dollar note. "You gonna ring up the lady's chocolate, or you gonna just stare at me."

The old man just trembled in front of him and shook his head. "Don't bite me."

Chuck was a statue of disgust.

The door opened behind us and the low snarl of the oncoming storm slipped through. But it wasn't the only thing. I turned and glanced over my shoulder as three of the biggest dudes I'd ever seen in my life stepped through.

It looked like a local football team had misplaced their entire defense. One of them broke away to use the restroom in the back of the service station as another grabbed three bags of cheetos.

"Everything okay here?" the last guy said as he eyed Chuck.

The mortal was a clear foot taller than the warrior.

"He said he's gonna bite me," the old guy muttered, earning a look of distaste from Chuck.

"Not even if you begged." The warrior cast the ten dollar note onto the counter and reached for Ava's arm.

"Not so fast," the big mortal snarled.

All I saw were bulging muscles as I lifted my gaze and stared at thighs bigger than my waist.

"Everything okay?" The Goliath's friend stepped from the rows of dusty crisps.

"This...*Vampire* here was going to bite the old man," Mr. Two cans short of a six-pack muttered, and then turned his gaze to Ava. "You okay, little darlin'?"

"Oh, Hell," I muttered as my best friend smiled sweetly.

"Why yes," Ava turned.

"This *guy* giving you a hard time?" The boofhead narrowed a steely gaze on Chuck.

"You got the wrong idea," Chuck growled.

"Oh, I don't think so," said chump number two as he stepped out of the aisle next to his friend. "Looks like you, *Vampire,* abducted these two lovely school girls, and now the old man behind the counter found out and reached for the phone to call the cops. It's okay old timer." The brute nodded to the pain in the ass mortal who'd started it all.

"You're right," Ava whimpered playing the part as the door opened behind the two brutes.

Judas, Bond, and Nero stepped through as All Brawn and No Brains number three appeared from the back and made a beeline for his buddies.

He was already rolling up his sleeves and eyeing Chuck as Ava turned and pleaded the innocent. "He asked me if I wanted a chocolate bar. I knew I shouldn't have gotten in the car with him. But he grabbed my arm and pulled me in."

All three towering brutes curled their lips and glared at Chuck. There was a cluck of a tongue behind us as the old man joined in.

"I think he hurt me." Ava fluttered her lashes and stepped in front of Chuck.

"Ava," the warrior warned.

But there was no stopping her. She just lifted both her hands, entrancing the three towering lugs. "Can you have a look?"

"Which one?" The main guy leaned in.

I knew what was happening, and yet I was helpless to look away.

"This one," she answered and out flopped a thick, heavy tentacle to smack against the floor. Another one followed, flinging out to smack one guy in the face; the towering male stumbled backwards.

Like a train wreck, Ava was unstoppable. One thick, squirming arm after another pooled from her small body.

"Jesus *Christ!*" one of them cried out as Ava grew bigger and bigger, rising up on her monstrous tentacles.

Her eyes changed color, turning blood red, and then darkening. "*Now, get out!*" she roared and the shelves around us trembled.

Glass jars fell from the shelves to smash onto the floor. The three delusional Samaritans turned, shoving each other out of the way as they hauled ass faster than I honestly thought possible for mortals their size.

The door slammed open hard enough for the door to crack. Judas and the others just stood to the side, watching it all unfold.

"You know, you really shouldn't scare the mortals." Bond glanced at the towering Great Creature of the Sea in the middle of the fuel station.

Ava slowly lowered her feet to the floor. "I know." One tentacle whipped out, snatched the two chocolate bars, several packets of chips, and salsa jars from the counter, and slid to her body as she strode toward the door. "But it's fun, and besides, they deserved it."

The old man just shuddered and shook, eyes so wide the whites were neon. "I...I, ah," he whimpered, drawing Chuck's gaze.

"Vamps aren't so bad now, are they?" the warrior snarled.

And the owner just held onto the counter and shook his head. Bond strode past me, and reached for his wallet.

"I got this." Chuck handed the old attendant another bill and this time he took it, carefully, while looking through the window as Ava skipped toward the truck.

I followed the others, shaking my head. Prejudice was everywhere, and Wolves and Vampires copped more than their share of hate.

But I still had hope that one day that might all change.

And hopefully no one would piss Ava off in the meantime.

I made for Bond's truck, climbed in as the others followed. Engines were started and we pulled out, heading back onto the highway.

Heavy raindrops smacked the windshield. Bond hit the wipers, smearing the dust before the rain grew heavier. We drove for another two hours, while the shower turned into a downpour, and when Bond finally turned off the highway and into a dirt road the once blue skies were dark and grey.

"We stick together, okay?" Bond called out as he slowed the four wheel drive over jutting rocks and a washed out rut.

The heavier the rain, the more brutal the terrain. I grabbed hold of the hand rail as the vehicle lurched and skidded and we slowly climbed.

"Not too much further and we're going to have to walk." Bond looked to me.

The car howled, tires slid. My heart lunged into the back of my throat. But I held on, one hand gripping the arm rest, and the other splayed on the dashboard.

"Bloody hell," Judas snarled through his clenched teeth.

"Told you it was rough." Bond wrestled with the rut, letting the car slip until the tires caught and we moved forward again.

Chuck and Ava stayed some distance behind; the grey sky darkened and we had to turn on the lights to see by. Until Bond swung the front end of the four wheel drive and stopped.

"We're here."

I looked out of the rain smeared window and saw nothing. "We're where?" I turned to Bond as he shoved open the driver's door and climbed out.

"We're at the Moors," he answered as the wind howled through the car, whipping his blond hair.

Behind me Judas and Nero followed, stepping into the squall and closing the doors behind them. I followed, wincing as the bright lights of the Hummer blinded me.

"No one comes here!" Bond roared, fighting the howling wind. "Because the place is haunted."

I winced with the word. *Haunted.* I'd had my fair share of curses and sickness lately. I didn't want one more tortured soul on my conscience. "Maybe you should stay here and wait for me?" I yelled at Bond.

Judas glanced my way, his brow narrowing. Pain moved into his eyes swiftly, just like the storm overhead. "Never, this is about the Blackthorne name too."

He didn't need to yell, I heard his words with the movement of his lips and nodded.

Cars doors were flung shut on their own under the gale. Bond lifted his arm and pointed to a small hill of jutting rocks. I blinked as rivulets of water slid into my eyes and caught the faint markings of a footpath.

The rest of the group lowered their heads into the wind. Chuck walked in front of Ava, protecting her with his sheer size alone. My boots slipped on the mossy surface, but Bond was there, taking my hand, his steps sure and steady.

Judas got to the start of the path first, he scanned the trail and then lifted his gaze to us. "It disappears into the trees!" he howled.

I followed the motion of his hand to the thin, worn path as it slipped between two towering pines, and disappeared into the darkness.

Something inside me clenched tight. *No, I don't want to*

go in there. Green and black consumed the view, there was no flicker of light. There was just...*nothing.*

Bond tugged my hand as Judas and Nero started first, slipping down the slick mud until they caught their fall. I jerked my gaze to Bond's.

"It's okay," he murmured. "I'm right here."

Ava and Chuck took one look at me and then followed the two Wolves into the small slide until the jutting rocks caught their fall. I gripped Bond's hand, and stepped with him, sliding before my boots caught. I strode forward, after the others.

The storm lashed and raged, growing more violent every second. *Something doesn't want us here...* The words lingered as the others pulled ahead, hurrying toward the cover of reaching branches.

Rain stuck strands of my hair to my face, covering my eyes by the time we left the torrential downpour behind. I sucked in a hard breath and turned to the dark, catching the faint outline until the path melted into nothing.

The faint sound of a child's laughter reached my ears. I glanced at the others, but none of them were laughing. "Do you hear that?" I glanced at Bond.

He frowned, tilted his head to the side, "No. What is it?"

"Laughter," I answered and glanced around the thick tree trunks.

Movement grabbed my gaze. A pale blur cut between the trees and disappeared. I jerked toward the flash. "Did you see that?"

Bond's gaze narrowed, but it wasn't turned to find the white blur between the trees—it was on me. "You okay?" He searched my gaze.

"Yeah," I said as the rest of the gang started once more, following the trail around the trees.

I followed, listening for that chilling sound of happiness that made my stomach clench and hurried after them, catching up before they reached the curve in the path, which then split into two different directions.

Bond pointed to the left, earning a critical glare from Judas. Still they followed, cutting through the forest until a clearing peeked through. Cold fingers brushed mine, before someone took my hand. I looked down to a child, a girl, no more than six or seven in mortal years.

"She'll steal you," the little girl murmured and lifted cold, soulless eyes to mine. "She'll take you in there and there won't be any way back. Not for you, not once you're marked."

A scream tore from my chest. I wrenched my hand from hers, and as the connection was severed, she started to fade, her intense, haunting gaze the last thing to disappear.

"What is it?" Judas rushed to me and scanned the path at my side.

I just shuddered, and jerked my gaze to his. "I don't...I don't think I can do this."

"There it is!" Nero called out, lifted his hand and pointed through the trees as he turned toward us. "I see smoke, and a cottage just through there."

Judas reached for my hand. The warmth of his fingers massaging the chill away. "It's your decision. You want to try to figure this out? Or do you want to leave?"

Nero lowered his hand, excitement fading from his eyes. I swallowed hard, and glanced through the trees to the faint white smoke.

"Stay or leave," Judas urged as rain pelted down on us.

Everyone waited for me to answer. It was more than my

dad's life at stake here, more than one tortured father. I looked down to the spot beside me and then to the Alpha's brown eyes once more. "Okay. Okay, I can do this."

"We do it together," he murmured and glanced to Bond.

They were always there for me, no matter what crazy idea I had—they were right by my side. I started forward and we walked through to the clearing, finding the worn path again. The cottage was small, too small, hidden amongst thick foliage and a mess of shrubs with bright pink flowers, the brown thatch roof and dark muddied walls blended in to the surrounds. If it wasn't for the white smoke, the place would be almost invisible.

"I'll knock on the door," Judas called out.

"No." I gripped his hand. "I want to do this."

He met my gaze, and then gave a nod. "I'm right beside you."

The others stepped off the path, letting us pass. I hurried under the open thunderous sky, through brushes that snagged on my pants as I headed for the door.

The rapping of my knuckles barely made a sound under the thunder. I waited for a second and then tried again, slamming my fist against the worn wooden door until the thing trembled.

One jerk of the door and Hell was unleashed under the guise of a young woman with the most intense green eyes I'd ever seen. "I told you before, I'm not interested in going to your stupid *fucking* Academy," she snapped. "So do me a favour, *and piss off!*"

CHAPTER ELEVEN

THE MOORS

"Umm, okay," I answered.

Raven black hair shimmered as she stepped forward and glared at the rest of us.

"Did you think if there was more of you, you'd be able to bully me into coming?" Her hand went to her waist. "I'd like to see you damn well try."

"No, I'm not here about any Academy," I answered. "I'm here about a curse."

She flinched and slowly dragged her gaze to mine. "What curse?"

But I wasn't here for games. "If you live here, and your descendants are Witches, then I think you know what curse."

There was a twitch of her top lip, baring her teeth.

Rain ran through my hair and down the collar of my shirt. Bond shivered behind me, drenched like the rest of us. "Can we come in, before we drown out here?" he asked.

A loud crack of thunder shook the ground. I shivered, hugging my middle.

There was a second where I thought she was going to

turn us away before she slid one foot backwards and stepped to the side.

We rushed forward, the shivering Wolves first, lunging toward the massive hearth and crackling fire. I followed Ava and then Chuck, making sure I was last and met the young Witch's gaze. "Thank you."

Power skimmed across my skin, raising the hairs on my arms as I stilled in the middle of the small living room, and the Witch shut the door, staving off the cold and the roar of thunder.

An old rocker sat in the corner of the room. A wicker seat big enough to sit three sat next to it, crammed with bright cushions and a purple throw, the edges frayed and worn.

"Nice place." I looked around.

"It's my Mom's, well...mine now I guess." She glanced at the others.

"I'm Morwenna, this is Ava, Chuck, Judas, Bond and Nero."

The others turned and nodded, wet hair plastered to their face.

"Crimsyn," she looked at each of us. "I guess I'll put the kettle on, looks like this might take a while."

"Thank you," Ava called as the Witch strode from the lounge room.

I followed, leaving the others behind. "I'm sorry for barging in on you like this." There were open boxes everywhere, some half packed, some empty. I glanced at bare cupboards and a thick stack of wrapping paper. "Are you moving?"

There was a huff as she grabbed a heavy kettle, and filled it from a jug of water. "Attempting to." She lifted her gaze to the half packed cupboards with faded china cups and a windowsill crammed with different colored glass jars and snarled, "You hear that? I'm moving, leaving and there's nothing you can do about it."

There was no answer...only the roar of the storm. My brow rose as I looked at the spot on the wall. "Are you talking to someone?"

"This damn house," she lifted her gaze to the small window that looked out to the overgrown gardens and turned toward me, heaving a heavy cast iron kettle with her. "The damn thing is stubborn. But it better listen this time, I'm done with its shit."

Oookkaaaaayyy...

I walked back to the fire, watching the others jostling for warmth as she grabbed a lever and lifted the kettle over the flame, securing it on a hook.

"You lived here long?" I searched the mantle for anything that remotely resembled being from this century. There wasn't much.

"Off and on my entire life. But my Mom lived here. She passed away two months ago."

"I'm sorry." I eased closer to warmth.

She gave a shrug and turned away. "I'll grab cups. There's coffee only, black, and I might have some sugar here somewhere."

"That's f-fine," Nero chattered.

I walked with her back to the kitchen and watched her rummage through boxes of packed containers of food. "I know I have sugar here somewhere."

"Do you know about a curse?"

She never even lifted her gaze. "Morwenna, I've been living with curses over my damn head for as long as I've been alive. I was raised with curses running through my blood. I'm sorry about whatever my great, great aunt did.

But like I've told the others that've come, *I don't know how to stop it.* And even if I did, I doubt you'll find the proper way to break it here amongst a pile of crap that's at least a hundred years old. I just don't know, *okay?* I'm sorry."

"It's okay." I stepped closer as she shoved one box away and started searching through another. "I think I'm more responsible than the words of your great, great aunt anyway. It's more like I'm the one who's cursed."

She stopped, and then lifted her gaze. "How so?"

I raised my hand, opened one finger. "Started school and found a dead mortal in my room on the first night, set up by a fucking Vampire bitch who wanted my family killed. Turned one hundred, was made an Understudy to the Ancient, Vlad Vasile. Was given Dragon Tears which I thought were diamonds to unknowingly take to the Ancient, and therefore steal all the Vampire powers of his clan, *almost* killing my family and everyone I know in the process."

She was riveted.

"Then had my ex-boyfriend and all his Demon buddies crash the school formal, killing students and teachers while they were at it, only to shatter said Dragon Tears and give everyone back their power. But *oh no,* it doesn't end there...then I find out my dad's missing, gone to the Blood Moon Academy."

She flinched with the name and curled her lip.

"And found him chained like a beast in the cellar, while he screams, thrashes and tries to kill me."

"Hell's sake," she muttered and took a step from the open boxes. "Here I was thinking I had it bad."

"A curse..." Pain slipped into my words. "That apparently originated from the Witch who once lived here."

She knew it all then, every cruel word, every hollow torment.

Every desperate need.

"I just want my dad back." I held her gaze. "And for all this to be done."

Thunder cracked overhead, like the Heavens answered for her.

"I don't know a lot about it. Only that this cottage has been in my family forever. Blood was spilled here, blood of my blood, and because of that blood, those who caused it will suffer for eternity. Mom wouldn't talk about it. Maybe it was her way of keeping me from it all, but I guess now it doesn't matter. I'm as much a part of this as you are." She smacked a box away. "The damn place won't let me leave."

I shook my head. "What do you mean, *won't let you leave?*"

"I mean, I've tried to leave this place twice. The first time my car broke down, right out there." She pointed out of the window. "The second, the job I was offered was mysteriously given to someone else, and the loft I was going to rent was set on fire. So now I'm homeless, penniless, and if this damn rain doesn't let up, I'll be carrying these boxes across the Moors through a damn flood."

I shook my head. "Your life sounds a lot like mine."

She chuckled and glanced to a box. "Aha! There it is." She grabbed the box, yanked it close and riffled through the inside until she pulled a small black tin free. "Sugar!"

I grabbed the cups from the counter, while she jostled the containers and yanked open a cupboard for a container of muffins. "Made these yesterday, it was almost like I was expecting company."

It was. Everything about this felt strange...almost *familiar.*

Ava glanced toward me as I followed Crimsyn back into the living room.

"Where are you from originally if not the Moors?" Bond asked.

"Here and there. I traveled a lot with my Dad, until he decided to remarry and have a damn life, so I came back here to live with Mom." She scooped instant coffee into the cups and then grabbed the lever for the handle of the iron kettle. "And then she died."

"Sorry for your loss." Judas reached out, holding the cups for her to pour.

She met his gaze, and then nodded. "Yeah well, the Mercer Witches never last long anyway, do they?"

The room fell silent for a second until she jerked from the moment, bent and handed each of us a cup filled with steaming black coffee, with the tin of sugar on the floor.

The fire crackled and popped, its warmth curled around my body like greedy hands.

"Feel free to poke around," she muttered and then glanced to me. "I've got more packing to do in the attic. I'm sorry I couldn't give you the answers you need. I wish there was more I could do."

She didn't wait for us to respond, but left, heading to the kitchen once more.

"She's strange, right?" Ava murmured close to me.

"No, she's nice actually. Kind of reminds me of myself."

"We can look around." Nero glanced at the open boxes. "We might find something we can take back to the Witches."

I blew on my coffee until it cooled. Ava heaped teaspoons of sugar into her cup. I stopped counting after five and just winced.

Boxes were opened, books and photographs were pulled

free. So, I turned to the fireplace and moved to its edge, running my hand along the cobblestone around the hearth. Judas was next to me, stealing glances my way as we ran our palms over the smooth stone.

And the moment our fingers touched over the hard surface, a prickling jolted up my arm. Judas flinched too.

"You feel that?" he asked.

"Yes." I stepped closer, fingers searching the grooves. "I can't sense it anymore."

Judas was silent. He reached up, massaging his chest. Pain and worry carved lines in his brow.

"You okay?" I stepped closer, catching panic in his gaze as it met mine.

"Don't," he snapped, drawing everyone's attention. "Don't come near me right now."

"Judas," Nero called out. "You okay, bro?"

But he didn't respond even when I touched his arm. "What's going on?"

"I just... just need some air. I'm suffocating in here." And he made for the door, yanked it open to an explosion of howling wind and strode outside, slamming the door behind him as he went.

"What happened?" Ava moved to my side in a split second.

"I don't know. We felt a prickle of magic on the fireplace and then he just kind of snapped."

"There's something strange about this place," Ava said. "Can't you feel it?"

I headed to the window.

"I'll go after him," Bond muttered and headed for the door.

"Me too." Nero followed, and the room was filled with wind and rain once more.

I waited, unable to search the boxes. Chuck and Ava did that for me, while I stared out of the small window, until finally a dark blur of movement came through the smeared glass.

The door was opened, Judas and the others stepped inside.

I searched the floor and grabbed a towel, reaching for Bond first as he met my gaze. "Just give him a bit of space."

And I didn't understand, maybe it was this place. Maybe it was us. I just wanted to find what we needed to and get back to the familiar.

We split up, the Wolves searching the boxes, but I couldn't help but be drawn to that mantle and the rush of power I felt.

"There's nothing here," Judas growled and shook his head. "You were right, we shouldn't be here. We're not going to find anything."

"We've only just started." Ava looked up from the floor. "You want to leave, then help us so we get it done faster."

He just glared at her, and then turned and strode into the kitchen.

"What the fuck is wrong with him all of a sudden?" she snapped, and then went back to searching through boxes.

I didn't know. I couldn't explain it. I moved through the room, running my hand along the wicker seat and then the wall. The place was old, older than I'd felt in a long time. The stone floor was uneven and chipped.

Ava pushed another box away, and moved beside me. "At this rate even that four wheel beast isn't going to get us out of here."

"Can you be any more dramatic?" Bond nudged me and smiled. "It's a storm and it'll pass."

"If it doesn't?" she growled.

"Then I guess you'll have to stay." I jerked toward the sound as Crimsyn stepped from a doorway on the other side of the room.

"I wouldn't want to impose," I started.

But the Witch just shook her head. "No imposing, besides there's a ton of boxes back here that you might want to look through. They're old, been packed up for as long as I can remember."

Chuck rose, rolled his sleeves up and moved past her, disappearing into the hall.

"So, you'll stay? Got plenty of coffee, and there's those muffins." There was something in her gaze, like she didn't want us to leave.

Like she was scared.

"Sure," I answered. "What could possibly go wrong?"

Ava raised a brow in my direction. "Wonderful. You've just dared the universe to make things go wrong."

I laughed and reached for her, taking her in my arms, hugging my bestie. "Never took you for being superstitious."

"You wouldn't believe the things my parents believed, like every doorway in our home was adorned with the skeleton of a seahorse as a good luck charm and to keep out bad omens." She shrugged and pulled free. "Guess it's rubbed off on me."

"Nothing's gonna go wrong." I picked my way through the maze of boxes to where he sat on the corner of the couch.

"Go talk to him," Bond murmured in my ear.

I lifted my gaze to Judas. "You okay?"

"Yeah, just this place gives me the creeps."

"Come be with us, where it's warm." I shuddered with the chill.

"I'm not...I'm not good, Mor. Not like I used to be. I just don't think you should be too close to me, is all."

"What? Where's all this coming from?"

He turned to me, and there was blood on his shirt, right over his heart. Blood that's seeped through the fabric. Blood that stuck the cloth against his skin. "Judas, what aren't you telling me?"

He closed the distance, grabbing my arms in a cruel grip. "I'm telling you to *be careful around me.*"

"I found Monopoly!" Ava called out.

But I just stared into the fury of Judas' gaze.

Until he released his hold and turned to the doorway. "Trust Ava to find something weird."

Yeah, trust Ava. I wanted to answer as he left.

Whatever was eating him wasn't something a board game could fix. I turned, listening to his heavy footsteps echo along the hall. But it might give me the time to figure it out.

I headed after him, walking along the hall to the cramped living room. Crimsyn threw cushions from the wicker chairs onto the thick rug on the floor. Nero added more wood to the fire from the towering stack.

"I'll get us more coffee," Bond called out, glancing at Judas, and then me.

"Oh muffins." Ava eyed the container.

"I used to play this when I was a kid." Crimsyn gazed at the board game as Chuck set it up. "Can't believe it's been that long."

A cold breeze seemed to come from nowhere, making me still...making all of us still. Suddenly the tension in the room shifted.

Bond and Ava set up the money, the cards and handed around the plastic icons for us to pick from.

"Okay." I grabbed the iron and placed it on the start. "Let's do this."

Five hours of laughing and battling over the landmarks, and I could have sworn we weren't in the middle of the Sommersbey Moors.

Nero was collecting everyone's empty dishes from muffins and a stack of corn chips and salsa that Crimsyn found.

"I won!" Bond called out, tossing the paper money into the air as if he was Scrooge McDuck.

"You cheated," Ava grumbled. "You made up your own rules. You can't collect rent while you're in jail."

"Yes, you can," he murmured for the hundredth time tonight. "Not collecting is a fake rule. If we had the rules I'd show you."

Ava gave him the glare of death. "You're just lucky there's no reception on my phone or I'd prove you wrong."

Chuck was packing the game away, laughing to himself.

"Well, that was entertaining." Crimsyn stretched, her spine cracking. "You know, you guys aren't so bad. But I'm going to call it a night. There's a box filled with spare blankets, you'll have to make do with these as pillows, and you might want to keep the fire going. It's colder than a Witch's tit in here at night."

"Thanks." I watched her rise. "I really appreciate you having us here."

"Better than roughing it out in the storm." She made her way upstairs, her footfalls light taps on the floor overhead.

The Wolves tackled the blankets and created a bed in front of the fireplace. They tossed a pillow and blanket on each of the couches.

I grabbed the board game and returned it to the book

shelf. I was stuffing it between two books when another fell out of the stack and landed onto my toes.

A sharp pain shot up my foot, and I grumbled under my breath, hopping on one leg. "Stupid goddamn thing." I swiped it off the floor and it fell open in my hand. My gaze fell to the handwritten page titled, *May 23, 1690.*

I flipped through what appeared to be a diary with browning pages, brittle corners that had long crumbled away. Selecting a random page, I read on.

After performing the task of feeding the elderly, I'm owed monies. But my boss refuses to pay me the shillings. He sees no proof, and he accused me stealing the food. Of eating it. I'm so mad.

Whoever wrote this ranted on and on about their boss. Guess people had problems with work even back then.

I kept reading until I spotted the word *magic* on another page.

My love has gone.

He wasn't mine, he told me, but he still comes to me. And tonight, he promises me love. Forgiveness, he says. But everyone warns me about the Warlock. He will be my undoing, they say. But I want to believe in my heart that he wants me too. Tonight, he will show me the truth of who he is once and for all.

I flipped the pages but they were blank. The rest of the diary was empty, like she never had the chance to write an update. What happened to her that night?

Everything of late rolled through my mind, the sickness, the connection with the Wolves and... I swallowed the boulder in my throat.

Was this where the curse on the Blackthorne Wolves originated?

When I heard the creak of the floorboards overhead, I

quickly stuffed the book back onto the shelf. What I'd read kept revolving around in my mind, and tomorrow I'd ask Crimsyn if she intended to throw the diary, as I would take it off her hands.

On the couches, I found Ava in one and Chuck on the other, all curled up like burritos, facing each other.

"You two better behave," I reprimanded in a sarcastic voice.

"Who? Me?" Ava propped her head up, smirking, and glanced from me to the fireplace. "I think that might apply to you."

I followed her line of sight to the blanket bed near with the three Wolves already tucked in, only their heads sticking out, calling me with their smiles. A spot waited for me between Judas and Bond. My clothes had dried, and I didn't have a change, so these would have to do. I switched off the lights and hurried to my Wolves, climbing under the blanket.

Judas collected me into his arms, my back pressed to his chest, and Bond had his hand on my hip, moving closer, sandwiching me. I looped an arm over his waist and reached for Nero, his hand and mine interlaced. Now this was the perfect way to sleep. Surrounded by three incredible Wolves and feeling safe despite our location. If it were just us four alone, I wondered what would happen if we started kissing, and more than anything I wanted to find out.

"Goodnight," I whispered into the silence.

Goodnights followed from everyone until we all lay basking in the fire's warmth and its occasional snapping sounds.

Outside, the wind battered the house, the rain slashed the windows. The building groaned, and creaked. I curled inside Judas's arms and closed my eyes, not wanting to imagine what could be outside.

"Sweet dreams," Bond whispered, and the exhaustion of the day flooded me, drawing me into the depths of sleep. I let myself fall, ready for a new day without rain, where we could head back to the Academy. I melted against my men and slept.

A sudden, ear-screeching scream erupted, and I jolted out of my bed, my dead heart giving a thud in my chest. "What the fuck!"

12

NERO

A BRUSH WITH THE PAST...

I STOOD OUTSIDE IN THE DARKNESS, WHERE THE WIND not only howled, but splattered my eyes with the beginnings of snow. The faint golden light of a fire flickered behind a window in the distance. And it was cold. So bitterly cold. I shuddered and rubbed my arms as the door opened.

She was just a waif, dark hair, green eyes, dressed in a thick heavy coat... *Wolf's coat.*

I flinched at the sight of the fur as she looked behind her and quietly crossed the front yard to a path.

This place wasn't home. Not my home at least. I turned, catching sight of an old stone barn in the distance. She was hurrying toward it, her steps almost soundless in the night, and the overwhelming urge to follow her consumed me.

"What the hell is this?" I murmured, but my voice was warped and strange, snatched away by the wind before it barely left my lips.

I followed her, keeping my distance until the quiet howl of worn hinges rang out. She closed the door behind her, leaving me to stand outside. The urge to haunt her steps was still there, stronger than ever, and it took me a moment to stop and ask myself.

Why exactly am I here?

The thought stilled me.

And where the Hell am I?

I tried to think, tried to understand how I'd gotten here. I glanced over my shoulder at the scuff marks in the dirt, but my mind was a blank. I turned back, and reached for the handle of the barn...and my fingers slipped through.

Past the metal and the wood, like I wasn't here at all. "Holy shit," I muttered and tried once more, but this time I stepped through, pushing past the stony walls to the darkness inside.

Muffled voices drifted through the quiet, and there was a faint light, barely enough to see by. I strode forward and heard her murmur. "Are you seeing someone else, Maxton?"

"Now why would you go and say something like that?" The deep male growl slipped through the air.

"Because...you smell like her."

The throaty laughter rippled, sending shivers along my skin.

"What the fuck, Nero?" I jerked at the call of my name. Bond strode from the darkness, confused, shaking his head. "Why do I feel weird?"

This was my dream, and yet this pain in the ass had to ruin it. "Because you're in my dream you idiot."

"Your dream?" He jerked his gaze to mine. "No dude, you're in mine."

I just laughed and turned toward the young woman and her lover. "Shut up you goof, you're ruining the show."

But the show still ran, whether I was watching or not. I could see her clearly now in the faded light. She reached up, wound her arms around the back of his neck and pulled him closer. "You don't want to lie to me, Max. You know how I get."

"I do, which is why I'm here, aren't I? You need to keep your word, your parents can't know about us."

She pulled away, the soft amber glow catching on her dark eyes. "You're still scared of them? I'll leave...say the word and I'll run away with you right now. We can be married."

"Soon," he murmured and reached up, grasping her hands behind his neck and disentangling.

I smelled the copper in the air, the scent of frankincense and pepper. She lifted his hand and the shadows in the barn seemed to swell. She was a Witch...a powerful one. I also inhaled the powdery smell of canine, of earthy tones. The man was a Warlock. He looked older, at least six, seven years older than her.

It wasn't right...something about this felt...*wrong*.

"When I figure out what kind of curse has wrapped itself around your family's bloodline, then I can remove it. Until then we have to wait."

She pulled away, pouting. "I'm tired of waiting, Maxton."

He chuckled once more. "You are a very impatient young woman." He leaned close, reaching out to kiss her long and hard.

Her hands fluttered to his waist and she moaned. I looked away, but Bond didn't, his eyes glistening as he watched. Fucking perv.

My vision blurred, and I rubbed my eyes.

"What the hell?" I grumbled. "What happening now?"

"It's your dream apparently. You tell me." Bond was squinting as the world around us shifted like static on a television screen, tearing us from the dark, cold stables to a crowded marketplace with people dressed in heavy coats and hats. The world was still old, with dirt streets, men on horseback, and carriages.

Snow fell around us, painting the stalls white and turning the dirt to mud beneath our feet. The sickening smell of cured meats, mingled with the stench of horse shit. I winced as Bond gagged and pinched his nose.

"Hell," Bond's nasally wine was grating. "Your girl-friend's back."

"What?" I followed his line of sight to the Witch, but this time she wasn't with Maxton.

This time she was alone.

The streets were busy, crowded shops and barking dogs. I watched the young woman as she slipped into a baker's store and looked at a stack of fresh baked bread on a stand. But she wasn't really looking at them, she was looking outside, watching before she moved again.

She was following someone.

I scanned the rest of the people, finding the man she loved further along the crowded streets.

"Looks like homegirl's a bit of a stalker."

"Really?" Bond jerked his gaze around and settled on Maxton; the asshole walked with another woman on his arm.

I followed her as she strolled through busy shops, hunting down her man.

"Where're you going?" Bond whined still pinching his nose.

"We're clearly meant to follow her, so let's see what's going on."

"I swear, Bro, you have the most shit-boring dreams in

the world. Couldn't we be car racing instead of reliving Pride and Prejudice?"

I kept walking, keeping to the middle of the street, until she stiffened and suddenly spun, before rushing straight for our direction. There was something different about her this time, something that made the hairs on the nape of my neck stand on end. Dark eyes flashed, sparkling with the kind of expression I'd seen before. "Nesrin."

"What? Where?" Bond swung his gaze, peering through the gaps of his fingers that still pinched his nose.

"Can you cut that out?" I snarled.

With a sigh he lowered his hand and searched the people in the street. "I still don't see her."

"I do," I answered. "In our young Witch's eyes. She's got that look, man. That look that makes you want to run for the hills."

"What look?" Bond focused on the young woman as she whipped her gaze around and looked right through us.

"Oh," he muttered, and then swallowed hard. "That look."

I'd seen crazy in Nesrin, seen someone pushed to the brink of hate when it came to obsession, and right now, in this weird ass dream I was seeing it again.

"We're ghosts. You made us ghosts? Get us out of here, dude." Bond shook his head.

"You think I wanna be here in this drab world? I want out as much as you do. But I don't think this is a dream. I think it's something else. What's the last thing you remember?"

"Chocolate custard."

"Really?" I snarled. "That's all you got?"

"Hey, you asked, and that's what I remember...and then rain. *A lot of rain.*"

A lot of rain, running down my shirt, dripping into my eyes. Thunder booming overhead. I winced, the memory returning in a rush. "The damn cottage in the Moors. You remember that?"

Bond stilled, brow furrowing while he tried to get that pea-brain of his to work. "Yeah, the Witch, Judas acting weird and Mor. We need to get back there." He looked around.

"Why? You miss checking your Facebook page?"

"Yeah right." He gave me a sneer. "Think you've got me mistaken with yourself."

The Witch bundled the layers her skirt in fists and hurried ahead. I followed her, feeling that same pull as I had in the barn. "Keep up dickhead," I snarled.

Bond mumbled, and then gave my shoulder a shove, pitching me forward.

When she came to a stop, I looked out into the crowds and saw him. Dark eyes, clean shaven. The dude looked intense as fuck. On his arm was another woman, small, dressed in a flashy dress with a lot of damn frills.

"Bastard's cheating on her," Bond pointed out the obvious.

But it didn't look like that. Not when you took in his body language. He smiled, patted the hand she had wrapped around the crook of his arm, but there was no desire in his eyes, no...*love*.

I wrenched my gaze back to the young Witch. Pain twisted her face into torment. She swallowed hard, and followed them as they walked. Her hand curled into fists. Rage prickling along my spine.

"She's gonna blow up," Bond blurted.

"Would you shut up. I don't need commentary." I was seized by it all unfolding.

"Yeah well, she ain't crying, and all I know is when you piss off a Witch, bad things happen."

I followed them, watching the young. Even Bond was silent as the Warlock and his companion strode toward a towering timber place. *Huntington Hotel.*

"Ma'am." One man bowed his head, nodding to the Warlock's companion and met his gaze.

There was a nod, the raise of a brow. "Blackthorne," he called.

"Hawke," the stranger answered.

"Holy shit," Bond whispered.

I was riveted to the Witch's lover, catching the glint of excitement in his eyes as he turned away. He strode down the steps of the Hotel, and out into the packed street.

"That's..." Bond started.

"I know who it is," I answered and turned my focus on the young Witch as she stopped at the corner of the Hotel, watching her lover climb the stairs with another woman.

I knew what was happening, and yet I was helpless to stop it. She haunted them, hanging back long enough for them to slip inside, and the longer she watched them, the more she changed.

There was no excitement in her eyes, no spark of lust. What replaced it was chilling and very...very...dangerous.

"Nero," Bond warned. "I don't like this."

I didn't either, but still I stepped when she did. My focus different now that we followed a predator. She kept her gaze down and lifted her hand as she climbed the stairs into the busy establishment and slipped inside.

I hurried, keeping up. The doors rattled as she passed. The men and women inside chatting and laughing suddenly stilled. A woman lifted her hand and rubbed her arm, and then turned her head to the rattle of the door beside me as a gust of wind howled. Others followed, shifting their stance and shuddering at the sudden chill in the air. But I couldn't feel it, I could only see the reason why the plunge of temperature.

Ice grew across the tops of the doors, and frosted the glass windows. But the Witch was already gone, climbing a narrow timber staircase as she followed her lover.

Her steps were soundless, but outside I could hear the wind whip into a frenzy. Glass panes rattled, and the building shook. If you didn't know better, you'd think a storm was coming.

But I did. I knew better. I knew the storm wasn't coming.

It was already here.

She stopped at the top of the stairs, staring at the closed door to a room further along the hallway.

The hallway around me blurred before I reached the top stair. "No," I snarled as the world slipped through my fingers. "Not yet...I need to know what happens...*wait!*"

She blurred in front of me, dark eyes narrowing as she turned her head at the last second, like she heard my plea.

"Wait!" I cried out as I fell into nothing. "He doesn't love her...*he doesn't love her!*"

And in the space of a heartbeat I was gone, lost to the darkness...lost to the void.

13

———

AVA

BETRAYAL CUTS DEEP

A scream tore through the dark. The sound made me cry out in terror and whip my gaze around.

Cold wrapped itself around me and gripped me tight.

"What the actual f-fuck-k." My teeth chattered as I stared at a small house in the middle of nowhere.

"Where are we?"

I jumped at the male voice and stumbled backwards right into the big lug of a warrior. "Hell's sake, Chuck, you scared the shit outta me."

But he just stared past me to the small house, his gaze narrowing as he took in the towering trees around us. "It's different, new...this is not where we are now."

"No shit," I muttered.

"You liar!" A woman's piercing howl came from behind the closed door. "I saw you! You were with that...that...that *bitch!"*

The male voice was a mumble, pleading, trying to calm the terror inside. I winced at the sound of her voice, hating the way it made me cower. *Don't fight. Please don't fight.*

The colored glass pane rattled in the window as the

wind whipped up around us, tearing right through my clothes.

"Stay close to me," Chuck warned as he turned, taking in the forest and the clear pebbled road out of here.

I shuffled closer, not afraid to take the Vampire at his word. "Oh, don't you worry, I'm gonna be all over you like a damn rash when this shit goes sideways."

"Willow," the man inside the cottage called, drawing our attention.

But the door was wrenched open, even though no one touched it. I jumped at the sound and grasped the big guy's hand. Relief swept through me as he clenched tight.

A woman strode through the open door, black hair whipping behind her. She stormed to the graveled road where the sound of a horse and carriage slipped through the night, approaching.

"Let's see then, shall we?" Willow said.

Hate filled her eyes. I'd never seen such anger, such pain, as she stumbled toward us and stopped to watch the carriage as it came around a sweeping bend and made for the tiny house.

"I knew she'd come." Rage stained her words. "I knew you were unfaithful."

The man lunged forward, grabbed her arm and whipped her around to face him. "Listen to yourself!" he roared. "Danielle is not my *lover. She's my cousin.*"

But the young woman was filled with betrayal and rage. She wrenched her arm from his hold and took a step backwards. There was something unhinged in her eyes, something that made my belly clench in fear.

"I can almost feel her anger on my skin," I whispered.

Chuck never looked away, nailed to the spot, just like I was. "Me too."

The young woman, Willow, lifted her hand, and the howling wind answered, bending the tops of the giant pine trees in the forest not far away.

"She's a Witch," I stated.

"That she is," Chuck murmured as the horse slowed to a trot and pulled up with a snort and a wicker outside the cottage. The door to the stagecoach opened and out stepped a woman dressed in white. "But I bet she's not," he said.

There was something plain about the new woman, dark eyes flitted from the man to Willow as she waited outside the cottage for proof of his betrayal. "Maxton." Her haughty tone grated on my nerves instantly. "What's going on?"

Willow whipped her savage gaze to the man at her side. "Answer her, *Maxton*. What *is* going on?"

There was a twitch at the corner of his eye. The horses wickered and moved forward. Still the carriage never pulled forward, the driver watching the drama unfold.

The air around Willow's hands seemed to vibrate, and I knew what came next. The anger, the jealousy, the revenge. I gripped Chuck's hand tighter.

"Not sure I can look." Yet I couldn't tear my gaze from the drama unfolding in front of us.

He slid an arm around my back, holding me close, and I clung to him.

"Maxton, who's this?" Danielle cut him a confused gaze. "She's just a child."

And those words only whipped the frigid wind harder against my body.

"Child?" Willow snarled. Her dark eyes glinted like an endless night. There was a maniacal giggle from her lips. "This *child* has been laying with him for the past three months."

"Willow," he warned and shook his head.

There was a flinch in the prissy-sunken cheeked woman.

"Cousin, this is Willow." He swallowed loudly, his words hesitant.

The young Witch wrenched her gaze to him at the pause. Her fists curled as she saw the obvious distaste in the other woman's eyes.

"You sleep with her? With this...*commoner?*"

The sickening snarl that left the unhinged Witch's lips made me want to back away. I held onto Chuck. Held onto him with all I had. "We have to stop this. We have to stop this *now*."

I lifted my gaze to Chuck. "We know how this ends, right? We know how this ends for *her*." My finger trembled as I pointed to the Witch incensed with rage and betrayal.

"I won't let anything hurt you," the Vampire at my side said, unable to tear his gaze from the events playing out in front of us. "But this is important. *This* is why we came. I'm going to find the reason for the curse." He met my stare. "And then I'm going to free my best friend."

My breath caught with his words...*his best friend*.

In an instant I became more than a horrible voyeur of another's pain. I became a friend, to Chuck as well as Mor. I became a fighter, a *hunter,* someone determined to find a reason for all of this, and to stop it before it claimed another they loved.

I stared at the young woman and saw not just the cold stony touch of rage, but the mindless hatred. She took here, and she kept on taking. Was it all because of love? Was it all because she wanted more than her lover was ever prepared to give?

I saw flashes of myself in Willow's eyes. "Let him have her," the words slipped from my lips I shook my head.

"Just let him go. It's not worth it, it's not worth all the rage."

The Witch turned her head. Dark, bottomless eyes cut right through me like this cold...cold wind. *Had she heard me?* Had I somehow reached through the void of this dream into the past.

I let go of Chuck's hand and stepped forward, calling through the nightmare. "Let him go, Willow."

She stilled, sucked in hard breaths as a flare of confusion furrowed her forehead.

"She can hear you," Chuck growled and strode forward. "Ava, *she can hear you.*"

"She's a *Witch,* Maxton. You cannot be involved with someone like that. *I won't have it,*" the cruel bitch snapped. "You'll be ostracised...*abandoned.* You continue this, and I'll be forced to tell our family. I'll tell everyone."

Agony tore through his eyes. "You don't understand." He lifted his hand. The tips of his fingers catching the faintest flecks of snow. A light pulsed there, white and soft at first until the power grew bolder, casting the glow around his hand. "I'm a Witch too."

"No." The cruel woman shook her head as her eyes widened. She stumbled backwards.

But it was the pain in his eyes as he looked at the blonde-haired woman.

The pain of *truth.*

The lying, blonde-haired foul woman whipped her savage stare to the stagecoach driver. *"Leave! Leave now. Be gone!"*

With the crack of the reins the horses lunged forward, pulling hard to the right.

"I can explain this...this *disease* you have." Danielle stared at the glow of his hand as the coach left under the deafening gallop of hooves. "You fell from your horse. You suffered a blow to the head. This is explainable, this is something we can hide...*if you promise to never use it again.* Swear to me. Swear to me you'll never use it again, and you'll come with me."

She straightened her spine, not giving Willow a glance. "I came here to show you what we could have together, as a married couple."

Torture twisted the young Witch's face.

Everything she said had come true.

"Danielle, you're my cousin...*nothing more.*" He turned from the Witch. "That can never happen."

The trees near the house bowed under the sleeting, gale winds.

A white fog reached through the forest to swallow the land in a frigid grip. It swirled all around us, consuming. I spun, taking it all in and stilled at the Vampire warrior. I saw pain carved deep in his eyes, the same helpless...tortured betrayal I felt.

I wanted to leave this place.

I wanted to leave with him and never come back.

I wanted to feel anything but this...this *aching.*

But as I stared at him the ground beneath my feet trembled.

"Is that what you want?" Willow stumbled forward. "Is *she* what you want?"

"You know it isn't."

I turned from Chuck, to the stony-faced bitch Danielle. She never showed a hint of remorse.

"But she's right." I flinched as Maxton turned to Willow. "This, what we have, can't go on. I can't risk my family finding out about us. There is too much at stake."

"Too much money," Willow answered for him. "That's what this comes down to right? To *money*."

"You idiot," I muttered as Willow just nodded slowly and stepped away.

I understood now. How can her love compete with power and position? How can it compete with the love and determination of another woman?

Willow just smiled and nodded. Her fingers twitching at her side, and then rose. But there was no faint white light hovering around her fingers. There was darkness...there was death. The sky above brightened, like the flicker of lightning. And in that pale glow I saw the mask that distorted Willow's beautiful face.

A mask of hatred.

A mask of rage.

And the air around us trembled as she let out a piercing, terrifying shriek and lunged for the woman. Maxton spun, terror filling his eyes.

"*No!*" he roared and leapt, meeting Willow head on.

But Willow's power was growing, morphing into a beast of its own as she screamed. "I curse you! *I curse you and your blood. I curse any children you might have and your children's children.*"

White lightning turned to black. I stumbled sideways with the ferocity of the wind. My heart was thundering, climbing out of my chest and into my mouth.

"*Ava!*" Chuck reached for me, grasping my arm as my knees gave way.

I couldn't breathe, couldn't fight, couldn't do anything as the ground beneath me cracked.

"Leave this place!" Danielle stumbled forward, fighting through the tornado of the Witch's power. "Leave here and *never* come back."

"No." Willow snarl echoed like a sonic boom. *"You leave."*

Danielle was lifted from the ground. Her feet hovered for a second before she started to kick and thrash, throwing her hands through the air.

"Stop this!" Maxton lifted his hands and drove his power into the air.

But he never stood a chance, not from her power...or from her wrath.

"Run!" I screamed, but only Chuck heard my plea.

And that bold obsidian power drove through the heavens like the point of a blade to hit Maxton. Danielle dropped to the ground at the same time as Maxton fell to his knees, slamming his hands to his head. Pressure built, like a vise was wrapped around my skull. I cried out, stumbled as the world around me blurred. Screams followed, shrill, terrifying and real.

Danielle stumbled backwards, her eyes wide enough to see the whites. She turned, grabbing the thick skirt of her dress as Willow turned on her.

She was going to kill them.

She was going to kill them all.

"I curse you," the young Witch raged. "I curse everything!"

She lifted her hands, her focus on the Danielle. Movement blurred from the corner of my eye. Maxton drove his boots into the ground, charging toward her. But she swung, turning that savageness into the man she once loved. His feet left the ground, spine bowed backwards as he howled in pain. There was no stopping her, no stopping what she'd become.

I caught Danielle lunge for an axe embedded in a stump as Maxton screamed, his face twisted in agony. One flinch of Willow's fingers and his spine would snap in two. His hands flailed in the air, desperate for purchase.

Until with a sudden *thump* the power stilled.

Danielle stumble away from Willow, her mouth wide, eyes filled with terror.

Embedded in the belly of the young Witch was the axe. A small, weak cry slipped from her lips as she stumbled backwards a step and Maxton hit the ground with a *thud*.

"*Willow!*" Maxton cried and stumbled for her. Blood spilled around the sharpened head of the axe.

"I only wanted to be with you," she whispered. "Just you and me."

He shook his head and reached for her. "I know...I know and I'm so...so...sorry."

Her knees buckled and she fell to the ground, her hands going to the middle of her belly. "You will be," she murmured, and he collapsed beside her, his hands going to her stomach.

She lifted her head and stared into his eyes. "What you've done to me will haunt you for the rest of your life, and when you die it will haunt the rest of your bloodline. It will touch everything and everyone around me. My blood." She lifted her hand slick and glistening in the night. "My blood will be the anchor. It will be the catalyst. From now until the end of days they will be forsaken."

"Maxton, come on." Danielle stepped closer, unable to tear her gaze from the young woman on the ground. She made a grab for his arm, dragging him away.

"*Get off me!*" he roared. "*Get the Hell off me!* Look what you've done. Look what you've done to her."

There was a shake of her head, the truth hovering behind the glazed, shell-shocked stare. "She was going to hurt you. She was going..."

"*No*," he pulled Willow close as she convulsed on the ground. "She only wanted to make me feel what she felt."

He sat in the dirt and the cold, pulling her to him as he rocked her. "Get away." He never looked up at his cousin. "Get away before I bury this axe in you too."

Danielle stumbled backwards, her hand rising to her mouth. It took a whole second before she turned and ran.

"I curse you," Willow's faint words mingled with the dying wind.

"I know." Maxton brushed her hair from her face and stared into her eyes. "I know."

There was a cry and a shudder. Tears blurred everything, and in this moment, it felt like I was under water, down in the darkest depths where the pressure crushed my chest.

I reached up, fingers winding around the base of my throat. And when I tried to find the betrayer...the *murderer* I saw she was long gone.

"Ava." Chuck reached for me, brushing his fingers along my arms.

I don't know how long I stood there while Maxton curled his body over Willow's and wept. He rocked her, rocked her while soft whispers grew softer still.

I stood there until the sound of galloping horses filled the night once more. Not one, but two horses carrying two men. They pulled their beasts up hard, hooves skidding against the gravel as the horses snorted and shook their manes.

"Maxton?" A man strode toward him, and for a second the past and the present collided.

"Dante?" Chuck murmured beside me.

The man looked exactly like Dante Livingstone. My breath caught as the warrior strode forward, but there was something different about him. He wasn't as tall...or as lean, and the square of his jaw not as hard.

"Leonard," Maxton cried out. "Help her!"

The man raced forward, and hot on his heels was someone else, someone who lifted his gaze to the air.

"Hunter." Maxton stared at the men like they could somehow try to bring her back.

"Livingstone. Blackthorne," Chuck murmured and stared at the men...and then lifted his gaze to me.

14

———

MOR

SECRETS UNRAVELING

I stood in a wasteland in the dark, and at first, I thought I'd stumbled outside into the cold night...

But this was like no night I knew. This night wasn't for hunters. This night was only for the hunted. A bitter wind sent a shiver along my skin. Darkness was a void around me, cold, empty...hollow, almost like I could tap this world and it'd crumble. "That's because it's not real," my voice echoed in the dark.

"About as real as we are."

I whipped around at the sound as Judas strode from within the dark.

"I think we're in a dream." He glanced around. "If it wasn't for you, I'd say this was a nightmare."

Brown eyes glinted as he stepped close. Blood soaked into his shirt, sticking the fabric to his skin, and a faint breath of anger swirled around him.

"You okay?"

He turned and looked away, not answering me. "We're in the Moors."

The faint howl of a Wolf rang out in the distance. Judas turned at the sound and closed his eyes, searching.

"Why are we here?"

He didn't answer, not at first. "I don't know."

I stepped closer and reached out, taking his hand in mine. "At least we're together."

He opened his eyes, and there was a twitch of his lips. "Yes, there's that."

He was acting weird…just like…the thought tried to find substance in my head. Just like the cabin…*no,* the cottage. I looked around. "I think there's supposed to be a cottage."

"There is," he answered and lifted his hand. "Over there."

I followed the motion as he pointed to a faint blur and felt a pull that hadn't been there before. "Come with me." I stepped forward, pulling his hand.

He resisted, until our fingers slipped and we lost connection. But then with a sigh he followed as I stepped into the dark. My boots slipped on mossy rocks. I stepped and balanced before moving my other foot. This wasn't the cottage I remembered.

Thick brambles snagged my jeans and jacket. Fabric tore and a sting followed, making me wince. "Shit." I reached down and touched my knee. The scent of blood was sweet and metallic in the air.

I didn't think you could feel pain in a dream?

I stilled as the question filled me, and then slowly lifted my head. The faint smell of smoke lingered, and with it the far away remnant of laughter. My laughter…*our laughter.* "I don't think this is a dream."

I turned to Judas who winced and stumbled behind me, one hand reaching for his chest. I lunged for him, wrapping one arm under his armpit to steady him against me. "What is it? Talk to me. What's going on?"

He lifted his gaze, and sorrow echoed through his eyes. "I'm sorry...I tried to keep you safe."

"Safe from what?" I raised my gaze to meet his. "Talk to me. Tell me what's going on."

And behind me the creak of a door swept through the dark. I jumped at the sound and spun. A warning growl slipped from Judas as his grip on my hand tightened as he stepped ahead. "Get behind me, Mor."

And the creak of the door ended. I stared at the old, decrepit building, finding smashed open windows and over-grown gardens. A memory surfaced, a cottage...this cottage with billowing white smoke. The laughter. That's where it came from. "I've been here before."

From the corner of my eye came movement. The moon seemed to grow brighter, casting a soft silver hue across the rundown building. But it was the shadowy dark figure from the edge of the building which gripped me as the woman in black stepped out into the light.

My breath caught. Judas stiffened against me. I jerked my gaze toward him as his eyes widened. "Do you see her?"

He couldn't look away, only mumble, "Yeah, I see her."

The woman in black, the one who'd haunted me since the diamonds were left in my room lifted her hand and motioned me forward. "Hekate," I said.

"Wait," Judas warned, but I was already slipping my arm from around him, already turning toward her.

"Tagar wanted to use her power," I answered. "He wanted to use it to slow the curse."

"Who is she?" Judas called out behind me.

"She's the one who's going to help me," I murmured and

kept walking as she moved from the corner of the building and slid through the open door into the dark.

"Don't go in there," Judas cried out. His grip lashed my arm, pulling me backwards. "Just *wait*."

But it was all here, all the answers, right within my grasp. "She's not going to hurt me." I stepped from the path to the rickety stone step. "She's going to help me."

I walked inside, listening to Judas' groan of disapproval; still he followed.

The forgotten floorboards groaned under me, wood cracked with the strain. I caught my breath and reached out, grabbing hold of the wall. "Be careful. The floorboards are about to give away."

"Careful about the damn floorboards?" he growled behind me. "You realize we're walking into our death."

But I didn't feel that. I felt as safe here as I did anywhere else. Shadows moved farther inside the house and the silver light of the moon spilled through the shattered windows. A flare of energy cut across my chest. I winced at the feeling and felt something in the cottage move.

"Mor." Judas' voice trembled. "I think we should leave."

I wanted to turn around for him, wanted to see why he was acting so strange but a desperate need pulled me deeper inside. A sob tore free, low, savage. I stilled as a blur of white swept across the hallway ahead of me. It sharpened into a young woman...*a young Witch.*

Power rippled in the room around her. Anguish filled her face, twisting pale lips before she spoke.

"He betrayed me." She lifted her head and stared into my eyes. "I knew he would. I wasn't enough for him. I wasn't what he wanted." She wrung her hands and stepped closer.

And that flare of energy in my chest grew stronger,

spearing through my heart. The feeble muscle gave a tremble and pulsed.

"I'm sorry." I took a step closer. "I'm sorry for your loss."

"His loss too. I cursed him, cursed this place, and me." Her words softened. "I was so filled with anger, still am...even after all these years. I can't leave, so I stay here alone in the dark."

Hekate stepped out from the corner as Judas called out, "Mor... Mor I think I'm...."

I turned, catching him sway on his feet. I rushed forward as he fell, but this time there was no saving him. This time he screamed in pain.

"The curse will take him too," the ghost said behind me. "It'll take everyone, even you."

I jerked my head toward her as Hekate pointed to the middle of my chest.

"I want to get out of here," I growled as Judas screamed.

I dropped to my knees beside him and pulled him closer, and for some strange reason it felt like this had all happened before. That death came for those you loved here. That this place was more than something forgotten.

"I'm sorry," I cried out and held Judas as he thrashed and howled in agony. "I'm sorry!"

"*HEY!*" Ava's voice broke through the dream. "*Mor, you need to wake up!*"

I opened my eyes to see her face hovering far too close. A fire crackled nearby. I turned my head, looking into the flames as the dream floated to the surface. "Where are we?"

"In the middle of goddamn nowhere...something's

wrong," she growled. *With Judas.* "With Judas," she finished.

I rose from the hard cottage floor as everything rushed back to me. Judas shivered and shook, his skin grey and gold against the ravenous fire. Pain tore across my chest at the sight.

"We don't know what to do." Nero sat next to him, holding the Alpha in his arms. "He won't wake up."

"The dream." I shook my head.

"You had it too?" Ava was a ghost in the middle of the room.

"What dream?" Crimsyn called from the edge of the room. "I don't know what you guys are talking about."

"The curse," Nero answered. "It has him."

"We have to leave." My desperation soared. "We have to get out of this place."

"And go where?" Bond snarled.

"The Witch's." The words spilled from my lips without thinking. "We need to get to the Blood Moon Academy...and we need to go there now."

CHAPTER FIFTEEN

PAINFUL TRUTHS

I cradled Judas' head as he lay on the back seat near me. Perspiration covered his brow and dampened his hair, but his eyes remained shut for the whole drive back from the Moors. We jostled and jiggled on the drive, but I held onto my Wolf, not ready to let him go. The car swerved on the next bend, and I grabbed for the door to steady myself.

"Careful," I called out to Bond who was speeding.

Nero glanced back at us from the front passenger's seat, fear crammed behind his eyes. "We're here."

I lifted my gaze and looked outside into the night as we drove through the open iron gates of Blood Moon Academy, reminding me of a monster's gaping mouth.

Tagar stood there, arms folded over his stomach, waiting for us with a grim expression. We'd messaged him about Judas' condition. And I held back the tears welling in my eyes. *Condition.* I wasn't a fool to think this was anything but related to what our fathers' suffered. And the Witch's words circled my thoughts like vultures.

It'll take everyone, even you.

She'd cursed our families. Here we all believed only the Blackthorne's were cursed, but we were wrong. My family line was involved too, and the sickness would come for me. For all of us. How long before I was locked in a room, chained up, forgetting myself and becoming an uncontrollable beast?

Dread thumped in my chest, and I felt trapped with no way out.

I looked down to Judas, wiping the beads of sweat from his brow with the sleeve of my shirt.

"I'm sorry. I should have told you to wait outside that cottage. This is my fault."

"It's not your fault," Nero said, yet I felt like someone had jammed a knife into my jut and twisted it.

The car came to a stop. Bond and Nero scrambled out, their doors shutting with thuds. My door opened and it was Nero who took my arm and helped me out as I gently laid Judas' head on the seat. I moved out of the way as he and Bond pulled Judas out of the back and Bond cradled him in his arms. He was the largest of the three Wolves, the most powerful.

"This way, quickly," Tagar instructed and marched ahead of us, his arms swinging by his sides.

Nero took my hand and we hurried behind Bond as they made their way down a dark pathway between overgrown trees. I could barely think straight from worry about what the Warlock would do with Judas. It wasn't long before we arrived in front of a small three-story building. A dorm. Most of the windows were dark.

Tagar pulled a key from his pocket and opened the door. We all rushed down a long corridor before the Warlock stopped in front of a door, and in no time, we entered a room.

I stepped inside and tapped the light on the wall as Bond laid Judas on a double bed. Only an empty desk and bedside tables filled the room.

Tagar bent at his waist, his flat hands sitting over Judas' chest where the blood had stained his shirt and spread. The Warlock mumbled words I couldn't decipher.

A light prickling of energy danced over my flesh. Magic. *Please let him be okay, please.*

It killed me to see all those around me falling, and I knew my turn would come, but I had to find a cure before it was too late.

Nero and Bond stood on either side of me, and they held me, their warmth keeping me protected. I adored them, and since first meeting them, we'd changed, grown so much closer, but we needed Judas with us. We were a pack, and even with one of us sick or missing, it left me shattered and empty.

The energy in the air flatlined, and we glanced up to see the Warlock straightening his back and facing us. "He'll sleep for now. Suppressing the pain and sickness is only temporary until we find the real cure. Come into my office for a hot drink and you can tell me everything about how Judas ended up with that mark on his chest."

"Mark? I thought he was injured," I murmured, but the Warlock was waving us out of the room and we closed the door, letting Judas sleep.

I looked back at the room, unsure how I felt about leaving him alone, but I had to find out anything I could from the Warlock after our experience in the Moors.

By the time we were in his office, each of us sipping hot cups of coffee from the vending machine, I started to feel semi normal. If feeling like I'd just been through the ringer seemed normal.

The three of us sat on a leather couch, facing the Warlock who reclined in his single seater, legs crossed with a cup of coffee in his hand. Bond reached down for the pile of chocolate bars he'd bought from the machines and opened it while we all watched him. It was the simple act of doing something so ordinary that had me craving normality back in my life.

"Tell me everything," Tagar asked.

Taking a deep breath, I started, and revealed everything from the clue about the Moors to Crimsyn to the freaky dream vision from the past. It still made so little sense to me that we'd been drawn into the past to see such a horrifically sad incident with Willow. I gave Ava's rendition since her and Chuck had returned to our Academy, but I left out the part with Hekate, and since only Judas was with me when she appeared, no one would know any different. Something inside me told me to keep that to myself.

"The Moors are steeped in ancient magic. Such a dark, dark place." The Warlock recrossed his legs, his gaze drifting to the ceiling. Light from the single lamp lightened the dark room, throwing shadows everywhere. "But I've never heard of anyone being thrown back in time or sharing a vision. Whatever was there, it wanted you all to see the past. To understand how the curse started." He swallowed loudly, and his reaction worried me. If he looked concerned, then what exactly had we experienced?

"It's Willow, she's a Witch and she cursed the Blackthornes and Livingstones," I added.

"That Maxton guy was an ass," Bond blurted. "He should have just gone with Willow if he loved her. If it was me, I wouldn't hesitate." My handsome, sandy-haired Wolf with blue eyes stared at me with a doting expression, and I leaned against him, adoring him. He kissed the top of my head.

"Sometimes things aren't so easy when family and emotions are involved." Tagar words were barely a whisper, and his gaze was elsewhere. His thoughts far away, and I wondered what happened in his past for this tragedy to affect him so much. Then again, it touched us all. Anger and jealousy had turned Willow into a mad woman, and it ended in her death. It shouldn't have happened, but it had and now generations later, we were all suffering from the repercussions of that day.

"Have you heard any stories of Willow or Maxton Blackthorne," Nero asked.

"Never heard of them," Tagar snapped.

A sudden and sharp ache settled deep in the center of my chest, burrowing through me like the worst damn heartburn in the world. I cringed and rubbed a fist against it, trying to soothe the ache.

The Warlock's gaze jerked, eyes narrowing and focused on me. He sniffed the air as if he were a Wolf, but it was more than that, I could see his ears pricking, the change in his posture to someone alert.

"I can sense her," he murmured as he leaned forward in his seat, hands gripping the arms of his chair, elbows poking upward. "Hekate!" he hissed. "I can feel her."

I squinted into the dark corners of the room, but she wasn't there. "I can't see her," I replied.

"You're sure," he whispered, glancing over his shoulder at the darkness in his room, his gaze flicking left and right.

The pain continued in my chest, and I reached for my coffee, hoping the caffeine might help with the ache.

The Warlock was leering at me, his eyes on the hand rubbing my chest; he was visibly shivering.

Nero and Bond both instinctively inched forward in their seats, a protective gesture to cover me. Right now, I wasn't sure what Tagar was doing. But it left me unsettled and uncomfortable, and a shudder raced up my spine.

His head tilted sideways, studying me. I hated the way he looked at me.

"Are you in pain?"

"It's nothing. Probably just heartburn."

He shuffled forward in his seat. Nero and Bond each placed a hand on my knees, like a barrier, and Tagar stopped short of reaching over to me.

"Tell your Wolves to back down. I'm not going to harm you."

"They have minds of their own, and I love them this close." I exchanged a long stare with the Warlock and something passed behind his eyes, something dark, and my instinct told me not to trust him.

He watched me. "I don't know how, but I think she's inside you."

I wasn't sure how to respond as it never occurred to me, but she had embedded the stone into my chest during my weird-ass dream when I'd had the diamonds in my room... I didn't want to tell that to the Warlock though, because any time I was under his scrutiny I felt like a bug. What would he do if I told him about the diamond from Hekate? More than likely, put a spell on me to extract it or something that couldn't be good for me.

I shook my head. "Only thing inside me is a dead heart." Shifting in my seat, I wedged myself further between the two guys who guarded me.

The air in the room grew thick and heavy. No one said a word for a long pause, then suddenly, Tagar stood and I flinched.

"It's getting late. It's best you get back to your Academy." He set his half empty coffee mug on the table between us and straightened his shirt as he marched across the room and opened the door. "I'll research the events and see what I can find to help with the curse." His fingers tapped on the door.

We got to our feet while Bond collected all the chocolate bars and stuffed them into his pockets.

I approached the Warlock who pulled himself taller until he was towering over me. "I don't want to leave Judas here alone. I'm going to spend the night watching over him."

"Me too," Bond and Nero responded in unison.

The Warlock let out an exasperated sigh and shook his head. "Sure. No problem. Just leave in the morning so others don't see you on the grounds. My assistant will care for Judas from the morning onward if he doesn't wake."

Leaving Judas here wasn't an option. It was bad enough Dad was locked up. But to see Judas in chains too would kill me. First thing was making it through the night and praying with every molecule of my body that by some miracle he'd wake up in the morning and be okay.

The three of us left the Warlock's office, and he locked the door behind us in the corridor. We strolled out, none of us saying a word, and I palmed open the door to the building. All I thought about was Judas. Bond and I trailed hand in hand behind Nero until we were all in the spare dorm room. Bond passed out chocolate bars and we sat on the bed around the Alpha. His pasty face was the same, and he looked as if he were sleeping, his chest rising and falling in a slow rhythm.

I inched closer and stared down at the blood stain covering most of his chest. "Can you bring me a wet cloth so I can clean him?"

Bond grabbed the spare pillow and peeled the cover off it before heading into the bathroom. The sound of water splashing followed. He returned soon after and handed me the cover, soaked but with the excess water wrung out.

"Help me take off his tee." I pulled the fabric up over his stomach and so many layers of muscles. Even while ill, they sat perfectly toned.

Bond lifted his head and with Nero's help we pushed the top up, part of the fabric sticking to his chest with the dried blood. Dread throbbed in my guts at seeing him this way. I tugged it free and drew the fabric up and over his arms and head. So much red smeared over his chest... I pressed the damp rag over the mess, wiping and cleaning him. With the material stained red, Bond collected it from my hand and took it to the bathroom.

I ran a hand over Judas's slightly damp skin, over the curve of his chest and stopped when I spotted a mark over his heart. "What is that?"

All three of us leaned in for a closer inspection. It was so small that I could barely make it out.

It was blushing red in color, surrounded by scratch marks. "Did he always have this?" I looked at Bond and Nero for a response, but both shook their heads.

"Back in the cottage when we first arrived, we felt a snap of energy when we touched the fireplace. And that's when he started scratching his chest. That's when he started acting strange," I muttered.

"That's a hex," Nero stated. "Mom told me people can tell if they're cursed when they find a mark like this one on them."

And I sat back, my face blanching. "So, the cottage somehow brought his curse out early." What about me? I felt perfect well, though part of me wanted to crawl into the bathroom and inspect my body for a similar hex mark. Though, I didn't want to know, didn't want to be reminded of what was inevitably coming for me. Not yet. Please not yet. I had to find a cure to save my Dad, Judas, and his father first. And then me.

"Willow cursed the family, so how are we meant to break a centuries' old curse?" I mumbled, fear shackling me in place.

16

AVA

MY HEART ON A PLATTER

The familiar lights of the Academy spilled out in front of us as Chuck pulled the Hummer through the gates. Any other day I'd feel a flutter in my belly, excited to see my family again.

They were my family. Mor was my sister, the Wolves, like brothers. I loved nothing more than to tease and taunt each of them...and Chuck—the nose of the Hummer pulled around the drive and parked beside the small cottage where he lived—Chuck was *definitely* not a brother.

He was...*more*.

The curtains moved inside a bedroom of the cottage. Concern tore through me until I realized what it was. "Jabba."

"Yep, goddamn pain in my ass." Chuck shoved the Hummer into park and shoved open the door as I grabbed the handle.

But he was already there, opening the door for me, holding out his hand to help me climb from the car. "You know, you don't have to do this."

"Why not?" Moonlight caught the silver strands of his

hair. Confusion crowded in, carving a furrow down the middle of his forehead.

"Because...I'm not Mor."

"No, you're not." He met my gaze.

My pulse sped as I stepped out and he closed the door behind me. The sound of a freaking tornado came from inside the house. The heavy thudding of feet followed, sounding like someone walking up the wall, and stopped the minute Chuck pushed his key into the door.

"I swear, I'm going to have a nice warm coat this winter," Chuck growled and shoved the door wide. "A honey badger coat."

Silence greeted us as he shoved open the door. Terrible silence that carried all the weight of a sword at the back of my neck. I knew how it must've felt for my parents then, when the chilling feeling of *chaos* was within reach.

"Where are you?" Chuck growled as he strode through the lounge room and into the kitchen.

There was a flurry of movement deeper inside the house. The warrior tracked the sound, whipping his gaze toward the hallway. "I swear if you've gotten into my under-pants again."

"Lucky badger," I mumbled before Chuck glanced over his shoulder at me.

Heat found my cheeks before he strode off toward the sound.

I closed the door behind me, and then turned the lock. Mor and the others were still at the Blood Moon Academy, leaving me to come home alone. Only the thought of that chilled me to the bone. I didn't want to be alone, not in that dorm room, not knowing Judas was sick...or that Chuck was alone too. I wanted to be here, to be waiting...out there I was forgotten. Out there I didn't matter.

"I can hear you," Chuck called from the far end of the cottage. "Why you little..."

My breath caught with his guttural snarl.

I lifted my head and followed, passing the table still covered with rolled up maps and hurried into the hall.

A torn piece of red peeked out of the doorway like a cheeky tongue blowing raspberries, strands of the frayed fabric hung from the top of the doorway. I took a step closer, and then one more. "Chuck, you okay?"

The floor in front of him was covered in shredded clothes...literally, I couldn't tell what color the carpet really was, from where I stood it was red, and yellow...and black.

"Oh shit, not my Armani suit." A whimper slipped from the big guy.

In the middle of the four poster bed was a once perfect suit, now it was just arms...and buttons, and in the middle of this *very* expensive mess was Jabba the Butt.

"I'm going to kill him," the warrior whimpered and lifted his head. "I'm going to...goddamn kill him."

He made a lunge for the little gremlin badger, but the beast was too fast, sending a squeak through the room before it leapt and scurried under the bed.

"He's ruined them." Chuck fingered the jagged bite marks in the fabric. "He ate all my clothes."

First it was his shoes. I still remember the holes in his heels, leaving pink skin to show through, and as he picked up a pair of black denim jeans I saw the same perfect bite mark right in the cheek of his pants.

"How can I wear this?" He turned to me, holding out the ruined clothing. I hadn't the heart to say I'd give my left breast to see him in those...torn underpants and all.

"You okay, big guy?" I stepped closer to him and lifted my hand, fingers curled, wanting to touch him.

"I'm fine...thank you." There was a glance toward the bed. "You must be tired. It's okay if you want to go. I'll deal with the little vermin."

But I didn't moved. Instead I closed my eyes and answered, "I don't want to go."

My heart fluttered at the words, breath caught. My body was heavy, weighed down by the mountain of terror I'd seen tonight, *what we'd seen.* "Tonight was pretty wild and I don't want to be alone."

He turned then, piercing me with those unfathomable perfect eyes. "You want to stay here...with me?"

I lowered my hand and swallowed the thunder in my chest, taking the bull by the balls...*or the horns,* or whatever that was...and stepped closer. "If that's okay with you. We can share the bed if you want. Just as friends, or whatever."

Or whatever? A bark of laughter ripped through my head, still the words kept coming, like an automatic machine gun fire of the ridiculous. *You're fucking this up, Ava.*

"I don't snore, if Mor told you that, only when I'm tired, or when I'm sick...I think I had allergies back then..." *Bloody Hell can you just...shut...the...Hell...up?*

Chuck smiled at my frantic chatter and took a step closer. "It's okay." He grasped my shoulders. God his hands were huge. "You don't have to worry about me, you just take the bed. Get some sleep my little Kraken. In the morning I'll walk you home."

My little Kraken...did he just call me his?

"Chuck," I murmured, my heart was thundering in my ears as I met his gaze. "I don't want to sleep."

There was a second where his eyes widened. Where surprise hit him like a suckerpunch to the gut. I could see the battle rage inside, where he fought whatever Demon occupied his mind. Make a move...make a noise...*hell, make something...*

"Ava," his husky, desire-drenched word slipped free.

Yes?

My breaths sawed in and out of my mouth, turning my lips arid. My tongue skirted the flesh, swiping against the cracks before disappearing into my mouth. He was riveted by the motion, and his own mammoth chest rose with a shuddered breath. "I'm at least six times your age."

My heart gave a shudder, stomach hardened. I could feel the tower of strength inside start to crumble. "I don't care about that."

"But *I* do," he answered. "I care about what people will say about you. *I* will care when I tear their limbs from their body at one goddamn word."

Rage brewed like a storm in his eyes. He was serious. He was dead serious. My body became alive. Warmth pooled between my thighs. I'd never wanted someone as bad as I wanted Chuck, and it wasn't the silver in his dark hair, or those cold as fuck ancient eyes. It was his strength, his untapped determination.

Or the way he fought that war inside his head. "I would...*give* myself to you," I whispered. "For the first time."

He snarled like a tortured beast and dropped his hands before stepping away. "Don't say that...don't ever say things like that, not to me. Not to someone...*like me.*"

"Do you mean, someone strong? Someone selfless and kind? Someone who is dependable and consumed with honor, even in the face of a naive, stupid girl trying to make the world's worst attempt at flirting." I tried to smile and ease the train-wreck of a moment.

He stilled as a twitch flared at the corner of his eye. And he said nothing as I slowly backed away.

"It's all good." I turned toward the massive bed in the middle of the room. "Just pretend I never said anything."

That tortured moan turned into a growl. I was grabbed by strong hands and gently spun. Cool fingers skimmed the length of my jaw, catching the tip of my chin and lifted.

"If you think those beautiful, precious, tender words won't play over and over in my head for the rest of my goddamn existence, then you're so very mistaken." His eyes bored into mine, searching, unraveling my desire.

He leaned closer, strands of long silver hair falling forward as I closed my eyes. The brush of his lips was soft, careful. I reached for him, pulling strong, granite muscles. I was nothing compared to him, just some small, insignificant girl.

And he was everything. He was power and lust, and...his hands grasped me under my arms and my feet left the floor, and those hands travelled.

I wrapped my arms around his neck and my legs around his waist. He held me like I weighed nothing and slipped his hand to the curve of my ass.

Cool lips warmed under mine. I speared my fingers through his hair and took his mouth. A guttural sound spilled from his mouth into mine, and in that moment I'd never been so lost and found all at the same time.

I broke the kiss and pulled away.

Emptiness sparkled in his eyes as he searched mine. Pale lips reddened by my hunger. I wanted to mark his body, to peel open that perfect facade. I wanted to find the man behind the mask...I wanted him. "I love you."

He flinched, brow furrowed as his hold on my body slipped and my feet fell to the floor.

It didn't matter if he never answered.

It didn't matter if he didn't feel the same.

It only mattered that I said it, that this school-girl flutter inside me finally had a name.

This was no panicked make-out session in the corner of my room. No forcing me to want something that wasn't there.

This was here, welling in my chest like an elephant.

An elephant that, by the look of it, just sat on Chuck's balls.

I swallowed hard and forced a smile. "Talk about a mood killer, right? Nothing like good-old Ava to fuck it up."

I turned, catching sight of Jabba in the corner of the room chewing on a silver Armani tie and then turned to the doorway.

I was almost there, fighting my way under a sheen of tears, when he spoke. "Ava...."

But I was already gone, striding through his house...dragging my heart behind me.

17

HOME IS WHERE THE TROUBLE IS

"HE'S AWAKE!" NERO CALLED OUT, AND I DROPPED THE towel from my face. I didn't wait a second longer but rushed out of the bathroom to find my Alpha, Judas, sitting upright in bed, running a hand through his hair, the morning sun brightening his face.

"Judas." I rushed over and launched myself at him, hugging him tight.

We fell back on the bed, and I laughed. I rolled over him, adoring the way he looked at me with his mocha eyes, all captivating and sensual.

"Why does it feel like I've been hit by a truck?"

Nero helped me back to my feet, and Bond dragged his Alpha up. "You passed out while we were in the Moors." He gave Judas a quick rendition of events since.

"And now that you're awake, let's head home to our Academy." I reached for Judas' hand, our fingers interlacing.

He didn't say much, but stared down to his bare chest where the wound from his mark had crusted over with blood.

"Your shirt's all bloody," Nero added, "and Mor cleaned you up."

He offered me a smile. It was weak and his face still looked pale, but nevertheless I took him being awake and able to respond as improvement. What the Warlock had done must have helped; maybe I was too quick to judge him last night when he asked me about Hekate.

"Let's go home," Judas murmured, and we were headed out into the corridor, the four of us. No one was about, and not surprising, considering it was just after six A.M.

Outside, a light breeze greeted us, and I rushed down the three front steps behind my Wolves, but my foot tangled over a damn branch. I yelped as I fell forward.

Nero lunged, catching me in his arms, and I was plastered to him, my face buried in his chest. I inhaled his musky and fresh pine scent and smiled.

"Why do you smell so good?"

He winked at me, and such a small gesture always affected me, had me burning up.

"Someone's still half asleep," Bond murmured.

I stumbled out of Nero's embrace, noticing my heel had popped out of my boot. "Give me a sec." With a hand pressed on the wall, I fixed my shoe. The wall felt icy and smooth, so I glanced up to the golden plaque nailed to the wall I'd grabbed onto for balance and read the engraved words.

Blood Moon Academy was graciously donated to the arts of studying Witchcraft by Maxton Hawke.

My mouth fell open. "That ass, he lied to us," I snapped, pointing to the plaque. "Last night he said he didn't know Maxton... Yeah right." I gritted my jaw, half tempted to rip the sign off the wall and storm back into his office with it.

"He's hiding something," Nero responded.

Bond was at my back, his hands falling to my hips. "Explains why he acted so creepy."

"Wanna go back in there?" Nero asked, facing me.

"You bet." And I marched along the windy path between the trees until I reached his building and pushed the door, but it was locked. I knocked, but no way he'd hear me since his office was down the hall, and I guessed his dorm was farther still. I sighed, hating that he'd lied to us when we asked him if he knew Maxton. How could he not know who donated the school considering the damn plaque was outside the dorm.

Judas placed a hand on my shoulder. "I think we should leave." His voice was soft and croaky.

I turned to him and nodded. "Agreed." He wasn't feeling well and he needed rest, so we made a quick path toward the parking area. I glanced back at the teachers' quarters, and farther toward the mansion like buildings with towers sticking out from behind the gathering of trees, thinking of Dad. Should I have visited him before leaving? But what could I do if he didn't recognize me?"

Nero grabbed my elbow and drew me down the driveway and we rushed to the four wheel drive before anyone came out and asked questions.

The drive went fast. I remained in the back with Judas, who didn't say much and looked like he might pass out any moment. I prayed he just needed more rest, but the mark on his chest had started bleeding again and he held two fingers pressed to his flesh to stop the flow until we could bandage him up.

"We'll find a cure," I said, maybe more to myself than to make my Wolves feel better. I hoped with all my might that I could follow through on my statement.

Judas placed a hand on mine in the seat between us. His breaths were raspy and heavy, and no words were needed. Just the knowledge that we were there for each other.

We pulled up in front of the main building, and it towered over us, blocking the rising sun. Since it was still early, I prayed the new school principal was still asleep. I didn't need him going all ape shit on us, not after everything we'd been through.

I climbed out of the four wheel drive with Nero and Judas while Bond went to park behind the Academy grounds.

The air was still, not even the trees stirred. We moved in unison. Nero and I held onto Judas, and the three of us rushed over the grounds. Not a soul was about, then again, most mornings students only emerged from their dorms at the last minute before class.

Being back at Bestias Academy brought with it a calming effect, like returning home. After moving here I'd changed, and this place with my friends felt like where I belonged, more than my parents' mansion, because here, I'd found myself.

Once we entered the dorm where the Wolves stayed, we rushed along the ground corridor. The walls were painted deep blue. Judas had explained that the majority of students in this dorm were shifters and the darker colors were calmer to their sensitive eyes. Because every room was taken, the Academy had to locate some students into other buildings. Must be hard for the cat shifters to live with white walls.

Inside Judas' room, the blue paint continued, matching his simple layout. Only the bare essentials—bed, desk and wardrobe. No paintings, no clothes all over the place, no left over chocolate wrappers as I'd seen in Bond's room; he had a massive sweet tooth.

Judas didn't waste a moment and had already climbed into bed. I hurried into the bathroom and scoured through the medicine cabinet, pulling out antiseptic and bandages.

"I'm going to get some food to build your strength, and all that," Bond muttered, sounding shaken.

"I'll grab an electric kettle and tea to help with the fever." Nero followed Bond from the room.

With them gone, I propped myself on the side of the bed, bending a knee in front of me as I stared at Judas, whose eyes were bloodshot. That small trip back to our Academy had been too much for him.

"I feel like hell," he croaked.

"We're going to find a cure." I couldn't even look him in the eyes when I said those words because on the inside I was broken, doubtful we'd find a solution in time, shattered to know I might lose my dad and boyfriend to some damn curse from ancient times.

But I pushed those thoughts away and cleaned Judas' bleeding mark, bandaged him, and fought my hardest to keep away the tears pricking my eyes.

I won't cry. Nope. I won't.

Judas touched my arm, his fingers curling around my wrist, the strength behind his grip weak. "Thanks for being so strong."

I lifted my gaze and when I met his heartfelt eyes, my damn tears fell, rolling down my cheeks. He reached over and wiped them away with his thumb.

"Hey, it's going to be okay," he offered.

I was shaking my head. "What if it's not? What if we don't find a cure in time?" My words shook on the way out and with them they brought an uncontrollable tsunami of emotions. They burst out of me and I couldn't stop myself from crying into my hands, my body racking and shaking as I imagined losing my Dad, my boyfriend.

This wasn't how life was meant to be.

Judas shifted in bed, then collected me into his arms, and I laid my head against his shoulder and cried. All the pent up feelings, the fear inside me came rushing out.

"Mom once told me the energy we put out into the universe is what we'll be given back." He cupped my face as I looked at him. "So, when times are dark, we send out positive energy, imagining a light in the blackest of nights. No more what ifs, okay, babe? We'll find a solution."

I shook my head and he drew me closer, our lips grazing. His mouth was on fire from the fever. He was right, I couldn't let myself fall apart now. Not when we were so close. The answer was right before us, we just hadn't put all the pieces together.

"You're right," I breathed and pulled the blanket up to cover Judas.

He slid lower in the bed and broke into a coughing fit as Bond and Nero arrived. I wiped my eyes and smiled, but worry marred their expressions.

"Everything okay?" Bond asked.

"Yeah, just so much going on. I might go and freshen up before coming back."

They both nodded before kissing me on a cheek, and I left them to care for their Alpha. I had to keep it together a bit longer.

I made my way to my dorm and up the stairs, but I walked right past my door and stopped in front of Ava's. I rapped my knuckles, waiting to hear her footsteps as she rushed to the door, but nothing came. I knocked again.

"Ava," I called into the crack between the door and frame.

Still nothing, and I didn't hear the shower running. On my way back to my room, I pulled my phone out from my pocket to message her, when a figure stepped from the stairway.

"Morwenna Livingstone," Principal Balefire barked.

I flinched and froze mid typing Ava a sentence, meeting the Hellhound shifter's glare. His angry eyes told of untold pain. There was tension in his rigid body, his tight expression. He marched toward me and every move he made was like a ticking time bomb.

Had he been waiting for me to return to my room?

The hallway seemed to press in around me, and if my lungs worked, I'd be struggling to breathe right now. I was in big shit!

18

———

JUDAS

SELF CONTROL... I HAD NONE

Sunlight speared through cracked lids. I inhaled, and then waited.

Waited for the pain...waited for the unseen goddamn cleaver to hack into my chest.

But there was nothing. Nothing but quiet and stillness...

And the glare.

I licked my lips and lifted my head from the pillow and the sheet from my body.

Blood crusted the mark on my chest. A mark I'd kept from the others....

And failed.

I hadn't been capable of much since leaving the Moors. So much for being a goddamn Alpha. I dragged myself around close to a comatose state, I might as well be in six-feet under.

Mor...

She filled my mind and clawed under my skin. She was in danger, and so was my pack.

But the danger was all me wasn't it? The ticking time bomb at their back.

I slipped my feet from the tangle of sheets and dropped them to the ground. There were no sounds of the others outside...still too early. One hard shove upright and the room tilted and swayed. I held my breath, waiting for the world to steady, and then made for the bathroom.

I winced at the white tiles and turned to the shower. Today felt...different, somehow. I shoved my boxers down and stilled.

What the...

My body was alive...more alive than it'd been in a long time. Hard and ready, slick skin stretched tight and erect until it shone.

I stepped into the shower and hit the nozzle, and the hiss of the shower filled the space.

"You're close to death one day, and the next you're ready to go, huh?"

Steam billowed from the jets of water. I stepped underneath and shivered with the heat. Hard muscles tightened as I lowered my head, letting the water hit the middle of my shoulders. "Hell that feels good."

Almost as good as... Mor's touch lingered, gentle, searching, slipping under my shirt. I closed my eyes with the memory and my body twitched.

Her lips were so soft, stretching wide as she smiled. Fuck I loved her smile.

Heat rolled through me with the blast of the water. Fingers wrapped around my shaft, I gripped the heat, feeling the shudder of desire.

I wanted her...wanted her more than I'd ever wanted anything in my life. I turned and braced my arm against the wall and slid my grip along the length until the tip twitched.

I'd taste those lips of hers, show her how much I missed that mouth.

Hunger roared with every stroke. Pale, soft skin, deep brown eyes. I'd touched her in my dreams. Touched and kissed and stared at an eternity in her gaze, and I ached to turn that into reality. I clenched my fist tighter, fisting, pumping, imagining it was her hand on my body and her kiss tracing down my spine.

A guttural groan ripped through my throat. Any slower with her and I'd go insane. "I want you," the words were husky and raw as my fist picked up pace. "Don't you get that? I...want...you."

My fist was a fucking poor imitation, still in my mind she whispered...*and I want you, Judas*...my length twitched, body gave into the fantasy, in this moment I was hers...body, mind and soul. I wrenched open my eyes, staring at the crack in the tile as the water washed everything away.

My knees trembled, but held as I straightened. She invaded my dreams, my fantasies and my days. I couldn't get enough of her. I just couldn't get enough. "I want more."

I grabbed the soap, washed and then hit the taps, stilling the spray and stepped out of the shower. But I wasn't done, not with her, and it looked like desire wasn't done with me.

A knock came from the door of my room and Nero's muffled voice slipped through. "Hey, Judas, you up?"

"Yeah." Panic blasted through me like a gunshot. "Just a second."

I raced for my cupboard, wrestled with a pair of boxers and looked down to the damn thing still at full mast. My trousers were next as a shudder raced across my skin, like a damn fever. I yanked the zipper high and buttoned my pants and slipped on my shirt making sure the top three buttons were tight before I called. "Yeah, all good now."

Water beaded and slipped down my stomach as the door opened and Nero stepped in. "You okay, brother?"

"Yeah." I turned from him and pushed the goddamn tent down in the front of my pants. "Just in the shower."

"Feeling better?"

Was horny as fuck an answer? "Yeah, thanks."

"Had me worried there." He closed the door behind him and glanced at the sheets, half torn from the bed. I bent, still turned from him and winced as I grabbed the sheets and threw them across the bed.

"Bond's outside." Nero shifted awkwardly. "Thought you might've needed a hand with...keeping upright."

I sank to the bed and reached for socks first, slipping them on before I shoved my feet into my shoes. "Nah, I'm feeling much better."

The desire to see Mor drove me as the room seemed to tremble and tilt. I swallowed hard and lifted my gaze to my beta. I was still pissed at him, pissed he'd kissed her first, pissed he had to do it in the dark and in secret. I thought we'd had an agreement, nothing divides the pack, especially love.

Shit, I froze. Not the L word it was way too soon for that.

Not love—my heart clenched, driving the heavy *thud* through my chest. It wasn't love...*okay?*

Muffled voices slipped through the door as Nero opened it and stepped through. He lifted his head at the same time as I did, the seductive and familiar scent of the Vampire hit me like a blow to the gut.

"Judas." My name on her lips almost made me moan with desire.

And something inside me stirred. Something primal and hungry wanting to mark more than his damn territory...*he wanted to mark her.*

I swallowed hard and stepped closer, my gaze drifting down her body.

Her pleated skirt fell half-way down pale, toned thighs, with long white socks sitting over her knees. Today, she'd pulled her hair into a ponytail, and my sights were set on the slender curve of her neck. I licked my lips, picturing my fangs there, grazing down the sweet groove to the base of her neck.

Mor smiled, her eyes falling to my stomach as I worked the rest of the buttons.

"How are you feeling?" She closed the distance between us, and as much as I tried to focus, all I could see was the sway of her hips, and the way her blouse pulled tight, gaping around the buttons as she moved.

I'd have her under me in a heartbeat, fangs tearing the buttons of that damned shirt open one...by fucking one....

Jesus.

I sucked in hard breaths. Gotta get control of myself. Gotta keep it together. I forced a smile as I fumbled with the last button of my own shirt, trying not to watch her as she stepped closer. God, I was still hard, punching against my zipper.

Her skirt bounced as she stepped, revealing her thigh.

She was mine.

Those words rolled through my head, my Wolf claiming her as his.

"I've missed you." She smiled. "I was worried about you."

My cock twitched as she wrapped her arms around me and hugged me tight.

I drew her close and lowered my head, breathing in her scent. My hands trembled as agony cut across the mark on my chest. Doors opened and closed around us. There was a deep, guttural snigger and the Wolf inside me wanted to bare my teeth and send a warning.

This one was mine.

Nero kissed her. He'd kissed her and I couldn't put it out of my head.

I slid my hand down the small of her back and cupped the swell of her ass, pinning her against me as I kissed her.

"Judas?" Bond growled behind me.

I ignored my Beta and pressed my lips to hers. I wanted it to be gentle, I wanted it to be every bit as soft and slow as Nero's, but I couldn't stop, not the Wolf, nor the pain.

She stiffened and agony tore through me. *Don't hurt her...don't fuck this up.*

Her fingers trembled, dancing against my chest, and for a second, I slowed, waiting for her to punch my chest and drive me away. But she didn't. Instead she buried her hands in my hair, and opened her mouth.

A possessive snarl rumbled through me. I picked her up and turned toward my room.

"Judas, bro, we've got to meet Balefire in like thirty minutes."

I gripped her with one hand, fumbled for my key and shoved it back into the lock.

Thirty minutes was all I needed.

Thirty minutes would sate the beast inside.

And in a second, I was inside, lowering her to those sweat-stained sheets.

"Is this okay?" I growled against her mouth.

"This is...unexpected," she whispered.

I pulled away for a second, and stared into those brown eyes. This was all I'd dreamed of, all I wanted and yet...*was it hers?* "Say stop and I will."

"I say fifteen minutes," Nero snarled from the doorway. "And then we need to go."

I lowered my mouth to hers. I wanted to consume her, to know every dark deed she'd done before. I broke the kiss and leaned upwards as I gripped her thigh. "Are you...experienced in this?"

Her nails gouged my skin as she gripped my bicep. "I've done...things." She moaned as I slid my hand under her skirt and reached around to cup her ass.

With that Demon.

The Wolf inside me growled and his hackles rose. I could see them now, her under him, her fingers fisted in his hair. *Take her.* My Wolf demanded. *Make her ours, she belongs to us.*

Desperation had me gripping her waist and thrusting against her clothing.

My hardness rubbed right where it belonged.

She moaned against me, and that sound... Oh that sound had me shaking with need.

"Stay with me," I murmured.

"I'm not going anywhere," she breathed, clinging to me.

My pulse was a tornado in my veins, diving deeper and deeper through my body. And I forgot all about the past, my surroundings, everything. All I knew was her.

Our lips mashed together, and my hand fell to her waist. I pulled the fabric of her shirt and reached underneath, finding soft skin.

Her hand fell to my hips, drawing me closer, her tongue slipping between my lips. I fumbled to push the fabric aside and slip my hand higher, finding the lace of her bra. My fingers inched higher over the perfect curve of her breast, taking in all that softness...

She groaned in my mouth, and I couldn't get close

enough. Smooth skin tightened under my touch as her nipple puckered. I drew a calloused thumb across the peak and caught her tremble. "I could take you," I murmured. "Right now. Give you everything I have." I lifted my head to lock eyes with her. "If you want it."

"I want it." She held my gaze. "I want everything."

Her blouse stretched tight and wouldn't give. With a snarl of frustration, I yanked her shirt up, revealing the smooth white skin, and the lace bra.

"Ten minutes," Nero moaned from the doorway.

I pulled away from her. She wanted me...she wanted all of me, and somehow that was enough for my Wolf. Somehow that razor edge we were both riding dulled and slipped away. I sucked in a hard breath and swayed over her as the world around me came back in a rush.

"Judas. You okay?"

I stared at her, as though I was seeing her for the first time. "I feel...weird."

She shifted under me, rising onto her elbows. "Tell me."

But I couldn't...I wasn't in control. Something shifted under my skin, like the icy touch of a...*ghost,* and in front of me, Mor's face morphed into that of the Witch.

I shoved backwards from the bed. "What the fuck?'

But in a second, she was gone, and the familiar brown eyes of Mor looked into mine once more. *What the fuck is happening to me?*

Pain shot across my chest. Mor pushed herself upwards as I stumbled back and reached for my shirt.

"Judas, I can smell blood." She glanced at my hand and demanded. "Your mark...show me."

I stood still while she pushed from the bed, straightened her blouse and came closer.

Her hand went to the top button of my shirt and popped it free.

Her breath caught as the cool outside air found the wound. Nero stepped closer, Bond close behind.

The hex was turning back, small darkened veins reached out, like something foul and necrotic. I looked at the thing and felt that quiver of terror. "The curse has claimed me, and there's not a damn thing I can do to stop it."

19

———————

REVELATIONS

JUDAS SWAYED ON HIS FEET. WE ALL TOOK TURNS glancing his way as Balefire strode across the line in front of us.

The wound on Judas' chest weeped and stuck against his shirt.

The hex you mean.

I winced at the words. My body was still on fire. I had to fight to stop from shifting my stance and looking at the Alpha's body.

I could still feel his hands, still taste his lips.

Still feel...I lowered my gaze to the bulge in the front of his pants. I should've known something was wrong. Should've known he needed me, and that this was more than sex. Driven by the curse it was mindless and...trouble.

"I should have you all expelled. *I wanted to have you all expelled.* But it seems my hands are tied in the matter. Some of your guardians are mysteriously unavailable, and the board of directors are not keen on moving forward. Know anything about that Ms. Livingstone?" Balefire stopped in front of me and glared.

"No, Sir," I answered and met his stare with all the composure my one hundred years could gather. "I don't know what you mean."

I guess it was handy having influential parents in very high positions.

Balefire's nose twitched with the pungent scent of fetid blood and tried to not wince. But I could already see the catch of his breath and the muscles in his throat as they tightened, fighting the urge not to gag. "Seeing as though your parents couldn't be here for this meeting, I'm letting you off..."

A sigh cut across the room.

"With conditions—" he snapped. "A curfew will be put into place for *all* of you. Including you, Mr. Blackthorne, *and* your pack."

I glanced at Judas, catching him sway. If I thought he'd been pale and grey leaving the Blood Moon Academy, then today he mirrored the look of a corpse.

"Yes, Sir," he managed as Bond quietly reached out and caught his arm, holding him steady.

"Curfews and escorts," Balefire snapped at me. "To and from classes. You won't be able to look sideways without me knowing about it."

Great...*just great.*

"Now out," the Principal snapped. Ava was the first to move, her face a mask. She'd not spoken to me, kept quiet and to herself.

"Hey." I caught her arm as she strode through Balefire's door and out into the hall. "What's going on?"

She just shook her head. "Nothing, I'm fine." Her blue eyes shone with pain, deep seated pain...*heart pain.*

"Talk to me." I glanced over my shoulder at the others as

Judas stumbled out of the Principal's office, anguish filled his gaze.

We were all stumbling after the Witch's cottage, all falling apart at the seams, and I had no idea how to keep us together. Ava just turned and walked away, leaving me staring after her.

"What's up with her?" Nero stopped beside me.

"I wish I knew."

Ava lowered her head and scuffed her shoes as she walked. She shoved one hand into the pocket of her sweater and reached up with the other, flicking the hood over her head as though she just wanted to disappear. She did, turning the corner as a guard followed ten steps behind her.

"Move." The savage snarl came from my right. I glanced up to the towering Hellhound, our shadow. "Class is that way."

Balefire just watched us in the distance, his lips curling into a smirk and then turned and headed in the opposite direction.

I glanced along the corridor and then moved with the Wolves, heading toward class. We'd spent enough time in Balefire's office getting yelled at. It seemed our little trip hadn't gone unnoticed like we'd hoped, and instead had resulted in a full-scale operation.

I followed Nero and the others to our first class, Creatures of the Sea, stepped into the room and found my seat.

"Nice of you to join us." Mr. Urie lowered the text book in his hand as the guard closed the door behind us, and then he continued, "As I was saying."

But my mind was elsewhere. I glanced at Judas as he dropped his pack on the floor and sprawled his body across his desk.

I couldn't stop thinking of Willow and the dream...or Judas.

Blood Moon Academy was graciously donated to the arts of studying Witchcraft by Maxton Hawke.

Or the damn lies. Tagar had known about the origin of the curse all along. So why hide it? Why let me believe he was the innocent here? Something about it wore at my nerves, like a thorn in my shoe I just couldn't find.

He betrayed me. The young Witch's words filled me. *I knew he would. I wasn't enough for him. I wasn't what he wanted.* I winced at the sound, and then glanced to Judas. A sheen of sweat glistened across his brow as he lifted his head from his arms and looked at me.

You okay? He mouthed the words. I wanted to smile and nod, wanted to lie.

But the classroom darkened. Through the window grey clouds seemed to move in.

"He betrayed me." I flinched at the voice next to me and jerked my gaze to Willow suddenly standing there, looking across the classroom to the world outside. "And he'll betray you too."

I shoved up from the seat, drawing the teacher's glare. "Ms. Livingstone."

Pain cut across my chest, like the tip of a knife carved deep and panic followed. Nero started to rise as I shook my head and stumbled backwards. "I'm okay," I gasped and then winced. "Sorry...I need to..."

"Just go, Ms. Livingstone," the teacher snarled.

I stumbled for the door, leaving everything behind. The Hellhound guard was waiting, striding forward the moment I moved through the classroom door.

"Where are you going?" The guard stepped in front of me.

I never answered, never even lifted my head. Agony tore across my chest and then speared through my body to my thigh. A whimper tore free, guttural and raw. I slammed my hand against my chest and the pain flared deeper as I staggered for the door.

Something was happening to me. Something...I couldn't control.

"Hey." Cruel hands wrenched me around until I stared into the burning eyes of the Hellhound. "*I said,* where the Hell are you going? You shouldn't be out of class."

And that agony morphed into panic and pain, punching through my chest with the clench of my heart. "Get...your...hands *off me.*"

Power lashed the air, dark and hungry. I spun away from him and tottered backwards. I'd felt this power before, felt that savage need driving me. I wouldn't make them fall, wouldn't make them shift...not again.

"Hey!" the guard roared as I stumbled, and then lunged.

Hard, sawing breaths filled me. My heart was booming, cramming that alien sound in my ears. This morning's sunlight was now gone. Dark clouds crept across the horizon, like somehow yesterday's storm had hunted us down. I pushed from the doorway and lurched outside, lowering my head to the bitter wind as it whipped hair into my eyes.

"Something bad is coming, isn't it?"

I swung my head toward the familiar voice as Ava stood from the bench seat outside. Her cheeks glistened, eyes were red. The sight hurt me more than the dark power ever could. "Ava?"

Something scurried away in the corner of my eye. I caught the white fluffy tail, and the smear of blood the demon bunny left behind. Those things still lingered on campus.

"What are you doing? Why are you crying?"

Ava just shook her head as fresh tears fell. "It's nothing." She sniffed and swiped the back of her hand across her cheek. "Stupid really."

"Nothing is stupid," I growled and then swallowed a wince. "Not if it upsets you. Talk to me."

Only then did she lift her gaze to mine, and then she looked at my fist pressed against my chest. "What's going on with you?"

I shook my head as the tip of an unseen razor carved along the inside of my thigh. My knees trembled, and then buckled. But Ava was there, rushing toward me, grasping my arms.

"Mor? Mor, what is it?"

And the heady scent of my own blood slipped through the air. I glanced down at the same time as Ava to see a dark red trail slip along the inside of my thigh.

I held onto her and lifted my gaze to hers. "I don't know that's happening."

"Come on, we've got to get you inside." She tugged my arm, pulling me toward our dorm. I tried to walk with my thighs closed, to stop the bleeding.

The dorm was empty, and for that I was grateful. I looked down as Ava shoved the front door wide and I saw the trail of blood roll lower on my leg.

White, hot pain burned into my thigh. I dropped my hand from my chest, and pressed my skirt between my legs as we stumbled inside and raced for the stairs.

"It's happening, isn't it?"

I jerked my head toward the sound as Crimsyn rose from the sofa in the foyer. She glanced at Ava and then my hand trapped between my legs. "The curse has claimed two more."

"What are you doing here? And what do you mean?" Ava jerked her gaze from me to Crimsyn. "What do you mean *the curse has claimed two more?*"

And the wound on Judas' chest drifted to the surface of my mind. I looked down, moving the hemline of my skirt higher. Thick red lines carved a circle on the inside of my thigh, and in the middle was the same mark...a mark of anguish...a mark of a Witch.

"No." Ava dropped her hand and took a step backwards shaking her head. "That's not happening. Not to you. I can't lose you, not you...not you too..."

And that feral power carved a line through my chest. The windows rattled, the small table shuddered.

"What the Hell is that?" Crimsyn cast a panicked gaze across the room.

"That's me," I answered and met the Witch's gaze. "That's the power inside me."

Crimsyn stared at that point in the middle of my chest and took a step forward. There was a wince before she lifted her hand. "I didn't really tell you the truth before. My family are Witches of the most dangerous kind. They are Witches who draw energy from the moon and the animals, and from dark, powerful things...like you." She lifted her gaze and murmured. "All the Dragon Tears were shattered, weren't they?"

"*What?*" Ava growled.

She knew about the Diamonds, knew about the curse. I could see it in her eyes, and now she knew my secret.

"They weren't, were they?" she murmured. "They weren't all destroyed."

The mark on my thigh stung and burned, tearing downwards. I cried out and reached for Ava.

"That's enough," Ava growled and grasped me. "You either help us figure this out, or *get the Hell out.*"

I'd never seen Ava so angry, she swept my arm over her shoulders and grasped my waist, walking me toward the stairs. Together we climbed the steps one at a time before I dug into my pocket for my key and handed it over. "Thank you," I muttered.

She was always dealing with my shit and never sharing her own. I wanted to change that. I wanted to be more than someone always reacting to the world around me. I wanted to be like her, strong and selfless. "I love you, you know? Whatever you're going through we *will* work it out together. I'm here for you, just as you're here for me."

She twisted the handle and shoved the door wide. "I know that," she answered. "That's the only thing that's keeping me going. It's the reason why I'm here."

I held onto her arm and stepped inside as footsteps sounded behind us. I made for the bathroom, dropping my pack and tore off my jacket.

"Show me." Crimsyn followed Ava inside and closed the door. "I can feel it, and I'm not the only one."

And through the glass doors to my balcony I caught the flicker of lightning.

"Why are you here?" I shook my head. "And how did you find us?"

"I didn't mean to." She turned and strode toward me. "But you're connected, I'm connected, this is all meant to be, don't you feel that?"

I shook my head as the pain in my chest grew tighter, morphing into a beast of its own. Light flared through my mind, and Crimsyn's gasp drew my focus.

"Your chest," she whispered, jerking her eyes to mine.

"Something is in your chest. I can feel it, it's dark and powerful. Magic, like I've never felt before."

Outside, the storm answered with a *boom!*

In the flicker of blinding light, I saw her standing outside, the woman dressed in black, Hekate. She held up her hand and carved in the center was a pentacle. "It's her," I whispered. "Hekate is here."

Crimsyn whipped her head around, searching. "Where?" she cried. "I don't see her."

She couldn't, only I could. Hekate took a step, passing through the closed balcony doors and lifted her hand, motioning for me to come. "She wants...she wants me to go with her."

"Don't go," Ava warned. "We don't know what she wants."

"She's here to help us." Crimsyn stepped closer. "Don't you see? This is all connected. It's why I'm here, why I woke this morning and just got in my car. She's calling us here, Morwenna. Calling us to you."

Hekate strode toward the door, soundless. There was a part of me that wanted to turn and run, to hide from this all. Instead I stepped toward her and the pain cut across my chest more brutal than anything I'd ever felt before.

"We end this," Crismsyn growled. "Once and for all."

The face of my father came to me as Hekate stepped through my bedroom door.

I reached out, taking Ava's hand, and followed, pushing all the fear and pain aside. For this moment I was the one they needed...the one to finally break the curse.

20

A STORM LIKE NO OTHER

I shoved through the door from my dorm and stepped out into the storm.

Lightning lashed the sky like the Heavens were filled with rage, and wind whipped the trees into a frenzy.

"Morwenna!" Judas roared and stumbled toward me. His eyes were wide, shirt bloody against his chest.

In the distance the howling wind blew the double doors on the main building wide with a *bang*. I flinched and took a step toward Hekate standing in the middle of the pavement.

She waited for no one, raising her hands to the sky, calling forth the rage and the fury. White light flared overhead, and the air around me rumbled with thunder. Rain smacked my cheek, one slow drop after another, until the bruised clouds opened up and unleashed the downpour, pasting hair to my face.

I lifted my hand to my chest and took a step forward.

"Mor...*no!*" Ava shouted and shook her head, heavy drops pummeled her face and slipped over her lips. She lifted her gaze and stiffened.

"Ava!" Chuck roared and hurtled his body across the empty space, head down, fighting the wind.

Still Hekate called to the night and as Judas battled to get to me, and Chuck to Ava, the sky split down the middle. The white light was blinding. I flinched from the glare and cast my gaze to the ground and behind me came the faint voice of my father.

"Morwenna?"

I spun as Dad stumbled out of an opening in the distance and fell to his knees.

"Dad!" I started for him.

"Mor, *no!*" Judas was there, grasping my body and pulling me close. "Don't go near him. He can't be trusted."

Brown eyes blazed with the truth as I lifted my gaze to Judas. "He's my dad."

Hekate lifted her hand as Dad lunged toward me. A savage snarl tore from his lips, claws slashed the air toward me.

"Dante, *no.*" Tagar raced after my father, sucking in hard breaths. "Don't do this, *she's your daughter.*"

Deep, bloody scratches covered his cheek. I glanced from the High Priest of the Blood Moon Coven to my dad. "He escaped?"

"I tried to stop him..." the High Priest lifted a hand to his cheek. "But he blindsided me."

"*Boy!*" the threatening growl slipped from the trees. Judas stiffened at the sound and turned to see the source.

He pushed me behind him. "Don't move, Mor," he pleaded. "Stay still."

Blackened eyes, mutilated hands, the man who stumbled from the trees whipped his head left and right, and then sniffed the air. "I know you're here...I can smell you." Judas' father had come too.

And in the flicker of lightning the middle of my chest glowed. I stepped away from Judas, pushing his hand away from me. "No, Judas. They've come for me, don't you see?"

Hekate turned toward me and lifted her hand. But instead of the rain, this time she bought the flare of power. She was with me, flooding my body and my mind.

Chuck grasped Ava and pulled her close as I turned, finding my dad, Judas' dad, and then finally Tagar ... Only in the power of the Dragon Tear in the middle of my chest, he was no longer Tagar, High Priest of the Blood Moon coven.

Brown hair replaced the black, his features changed, hardening his jaw, and changing the color of his eyes. I knew who he was now, knew from the description of the others.

Say it...say his name, I flinched and jerked my gaze to Hekate, only she wasn't alone. The young Witch from the cottage stood next to her, her dark eyes fixed on the High Priest.

"Maxton Hawke," the name slipped from my lips.

Tagar paled and tipped his head forward.

Tell him. Willow stepped from Hekate's side and headed for me. *Tell him this was all because he betrayed me.*

"You betrayed her," the words flowed. "You betrayed someone who loved you."

He shook his head as the glamor fell away revealing Maxton as we'd seen him in the village, not the Warlock from Blood Moon Academy.

A gasp came from those at my side.

"That's him," Nero growled. "That's the sonofawitch who broke her heart."

"*No!*" Maxton stumbled forward. "I *never* betrayed her. *I loved her...*"

He lies. Willow answered and floated beside me as the wind eased. Still the skies rumbled and snarled.

"I tried to convince my family," Maxton continued. "I just needed time, needed Willow to understand. Danielle was the one my family listened to. She was the one they respected. I thought if I could just get her on my side, then they'd learn to accept Willow, and maybe even love her," his voice softened, turning cold and dark, just like the storm above.

I saw him, Willow stared at him with the cruel, unflinching eyes. *I saw him with her.*

"She saw you that day…" the memory flooded back to me like it was *my* memory. The choking scent of dust and horses, the wooden stairs creaking under my feet as I climbed the motel stairs and stopped at the landing, listening to their laughter. "In the motel, you were laughing…you were."

"Trying to get Danielle onside," he pleaded. "I was trying to get her to see how happy I was. I didn't know she'd come with other intentions, I swear to you, I'm telling the truth."

Willow flinched with the words.

Maxton's gaze stilled at my side, his voice shaking. "S-she's here, isn't s-she?"

I tried to not see the anguish in his eyes, but I couldn't, it was all there burning on the surface, reducing the High Priest to nothing more than a mortal man in love. "I thought…I thought I could give her the world. Thought with my family's approval I'd not lose my inheritance."

I didn't want money, she answered, her voice cracking with pain. *I only wanted him.*

"In the end it didn't matter," hoarse words tore from his lips. "I lost her anyway, lost my future…lost myself." He stared at the spot where she stood. "My life meant nothing without her. I've tried to release her, I've tried to break the curse she put on herself that night. I've tried to set her free. I thought with Hekate's power I might've had a chance."

I glanced to the Witch in black.

"I wish it was me who died that night."

Willow flinched as he sank to his knees. She took a step forward, drawn by something stronger than hate and rage.

Love.

The energy around her shimmered, growing brighter as Hekate turned and strode toward me.

"She forgives you," the words slipped from my lips as the most powerful Witch who ever lived lifted her hand and pressed her fingers to my chest.

"I just wanted her to be at peace." Maxton lifted tear-stained eyes to the spot where Willow stood. "I just wish there was some way to set her free."

"There is." I stared into the dark eyes of the Goddess of Necromancy and felt the depths of her power.

She was endless...infinite and ferocious. She was darkness and love and death all pooled into one. She was the air I breathed, and the blood in my veins. She was Witch.

And as I closed my eyes lightning slashed the sky above. "She forgives you, Maxton. She forgives you and she's ready to let go."

Hairs on my arms stood on end as the wind started once more, whipping around us like a tornado. And as I plunged into that power inside my chest and connected with something unfathomable, I felt Willow's love for Maxton carry me away.

It all made sense, the answer lay with me.

I was the cure to the curse.

I was answer...the answer to it all.

Energy coursed through the air around us, turning grey storm clouds black.

And as a crack of lightning coursed through the sky once more a storm was unleashed.

Only it wasn't a storm filled with piercing glare and deafening thunder.

It was a power storm...*a Witch storm.*

A savage growl slipped from Judas's lips. He took a step away from me, eyes wide, staring at me like he was terrified. But I couldn't help him, not now...not when I had Hekate coursing through my veins.

I lifted my hands and felt every dark, hidden *thing* around me. Every secret, every curse...and every spell crumbled under Hekate's power. With a sonic *boom* it tore across the Academy grounds. I opened my eyes to see those around me stumble. My dad fell to his knees as the pure white glow from Dragon Tear in the middle of my chest washed over him.

Gone was the tortured look of pain...gone was the rage in his eyes, in this moment he was my dad once more. Judas' father followed, falling to his knees and then bowed his head.

Blackthorne.

Livingstone.

Judas cried out and wrenched his hand to his shirt, tearing buttons free as he yanked the neckline, exposing his chest. But the mark was gone...the Hex that burned his skin.

"Willow?" Maxton cried out, and stumbled forward.

And in the bright glow of the Dragon Tears they found each other once more. He stumbled toward her, wrapping his arms around her tight. She held him close, slipping her hands to his face before she kissed him.

"I love you," he cried, touching her cheek, and burying

his face into the crook of her neck. "I've missed you so much...*so very much*."

I glanced to Judas who stared at me with same look. Nero fought the energy coursing from the middle of my chest to stand next to his Alpha, and Bond stepped to the other side. Love was all around me, in every gaze...in every heart.

Including mine. I closed my eyes, holding the faces of all those I loved in my mind and with all the power I had left I screamed, severing my connection to Hekate...

And shattered the last remaining Dragon Tear.

Darkness plunged around me...darkness and silence.

I stilled for a second, knees trembling before they buckled.

Hands reached for me, grabbing me before I hit the ground.

"I've got you," my Dad growled.

"*We've* got you," Judas followed.

And they did...they had me...they had all of me...

My heart.

My power.

I opened my eyes to see those I loved with new eyes.

"Daddy?"

He smiled as I spoke his name.

"I'm okay." he brushed strands of my hair from my face. "I'm okay now."

I glanced to Judas, Nero and Bond and caught their frightened smiles as they looked at me.

But behind them the Academy trembled with power...I could feel it coming alive...

Unearthing every hidden secret...

Revealing treacherous pasts.

A haunting screech cut through the air from somewhere on the grounds.

I looked past my father, to Hekate...but she was gone, just like her power inside me. Maxton held Willow in his arms, but she too was fading, falling away as the storm overhead settled around us.

"Come on." Dad rose to his feet, lifting me as he went.

"We have her, Sir...if that's okay with you." Judas glanced to my dad.

There was a second when I saw the man they feared, the man who'd go to any lengths to protect those he loved. But in the end, he just nodded and dropped his hands from around me.

My Wolves were there to take his place.

"Dante," Chuck growled. "Are you okay?"

Dad gave me a weak smile and turned to the Vampire warrior. "Yes, old friend, I am now. Ava, you okay?"

I glanced to my best friend, huddled close to Chuck with his arm wrapped around her. She glanced at me and gave me a nod. "I am now."

As the clouds overhead slowly drifted away, I knew the curse was gone...once and for all.

EPILOGUE

Darkness swept across the Academy grounds like the night was a silent predator, hunting.

Power lingered from the Witch storm.

Power that shimmered and shook the building's foundations...power that brought to life secrets better left dead.

Shadows slipped from their prisons.

Things that'd been spelled for hundreds of years finally shook loose of their shackles and took their first breath. Rage rolled like the remnant of thunder.

Monsters walked the grounds of Bestias Academy, while the Beautiful Beasts slept.

And at the back of the main building, the surface of the pond shimmered, casting reds, and blues...and yellows like an oil slick.

Out of that slick shot a hand, and then an arm, and with a shuddering gasp of air came a man...a man with yellow hair...a man with a mane that dripped as he pushed from the pond.

Golden scales shimmered, before they turned to skin.

He stumbled naked out into the open, trying to

remember where he was and looked up to the lights from the dormitories. And with a shuddering breath he dropped to all fours.

As the power drifted from building to building waking the nightmares of the past, he slowly shifted into the Lion he was.

With a savage roar he took a step, coated in soft yellow fur.

Hate burned in yellow eyes.

Hate fueled by retribution.

And somewhere in the darkness of Bestias Academy...something just as hated...answered him back....

We, at team Kila Foung hope you enjoyed something a little darker. We tried to channel our inner Sabrina, and bring you something intense.
If you'd like snippets and insider gossip, then please join out Facebook Group, Kila Foung Reader Group.
We're so excited about the next book comin' at you **1st July**. We're getting HOTTTT with the Wolves.
So excited.
Love you all. See you Kila Foung Readers to find out more.
But for now, stay sassy...and a lot of assy.
Lots of love,
Kim Faulks and Mila Young.

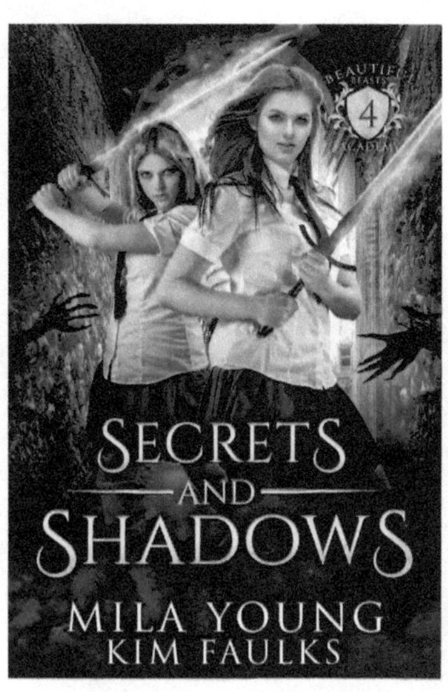

There's nothing like a witch storm to unearth a century of dark secrets…and there's nothing like a best friend with a flaming sword at your back to end them once and for all…

The curse which infected those I love is over…and the woman in black is now gone.

But Bastias Academy has changed since the Witch storm.

Secrets have resurfaced and shadows consume the dorms.

An old Principal haunts the hallways, leaving grave dirt in her wake.

But that's not all that's surfaced.

The fish in the pond are savaged and eaten….

And one is mysteriously gone.

A monsterous golden fish with bright yellow eyes, leaving behind human shaped footprints in its wake.

Ava takes refuge with Chuck, leaving me to huddle with the Wolves.

And as love and lust lunger on Judas' lips I find myself drawn into a battle like nothing before.

Lions will come.

Lies will be exposed.

But will love conquer all?

I guess I'm about to find out.

Pre-order Secrets & Shadows here today!